Ivy and Audie

Colleen B. MacFarlane, MA, MBA
and
Bruce A. MacFarlane, PhD.

www.colleenbooks.com

A Story for Teens with Epilepsy

Artwork and Design by Colleen B. MacFarlane

Customized Illustrations by Matthew Gonya

ISBN: 9798833595916

Printed in the United States of America

First Edition, Self-Published

DISCLAIMER

This book is fictionalized. Names, characters, places and incidents either are products of the author's imagination or are used fictitiously. Any resemblance to actual events, advice or locales or persons, living or dead, is entirely coincidental.

No portions or excerpts may be used in any format without the written permission of the author.

The authors are not medical doctors. The information contained in this book should not be taken as medical advice. All patients are different and struggle with varying constellations of symptoms; therefore, proper testing with a qualified professional is critical. Medications by name and dosage should also not be viewed as medical advice. Any person who experiences seizures should always consult a physician, which is paramount to proper care.

The authors are not dog trainers and have chosen purposely not to give precise advice. The authors are aware of varying opinions about alert dogs and how to train service dogs. Some of it is anecdotal and others claim to rely on statistically valid and reliable studies. Readers must understand that the authors are not making recommendations to particular dog agencies nor philosophies regarding training.

DEDICATION

This book is dedicated to all patients, young and old, who live with the diagnosis of epilepsy. Those who experience seizures on a regular basis show admirable courage. I salute all patients who meet their personal challenge with tenacity and resiliency in coping with this diagnosis. The stories of patients that I have read demonstrate a life force that embodies strength and character.

Secondly, I have deep gratitude for all practitioners of medicine who have dedicated their lives to helping their patients with epilepsy.

And lastly, I dedicate this book to all of our four-legged friends who are alert dogs or service dogs. They are truly man's best friend in a most profound way.

IVY AND AUDIE

As a miniature schnauzer pup, Audie was happy to be the star attraction in the Cole household. Audie embraced his job as guardian of the Cole family. Each and every visitor faced Audie's scrutiny, including his sniffs, and an occasional growl accompanied by his legendary schnauzer bark. All of Audie's days were filled with running, staring out the front window while sitting on top of the couch, and tilting his head to the left every time Mrs. Cole spoke to him in her friendly, raised voice. "Come here, Audie, wanna treat? Good boy." Audie happily gobbled down his favorite beef nugget, then hung around mama Cole for an extra scratch behind the ears.

Charlotte Cole was the mother of the household and Donovan Cole was her husband. Their eight-year-old son, Gunner, was their only child. Audie depended on Gunner for his daily rough-housing that was always followed by lots of belly rubs. Audie saw Gunner off to school every day and eagerly awaited his return from school each afternoon. Audie's tail predictably went a-wagging when he heard one of the family members raise the pitch in their voice, as he knew his favorite treat or a petting was soon on its way. The minute Gunner came home from school, Audie was at the door, waiting to start his ritual of sloppy love-licks once Gunner's face was within reach. Gunner was only too happy to get a good soaking on his freckled face. Donovan had hinted to Gunner that someday Audie might actually lick all the freckles off his face. Gunner wasn't sure if this was possible, but he thought it might be.

Little did Audie know that his life was about to change. Audie would soon be required to perform a very important task in the Cole household. His new role was going to be invaluable to a nine-year-old girl. Her name was Ivy, and she was Gunner's cousin. Ivy lived two doors from the Cole's. Ivy and Gunner had been best buds since either of them could remember.

IVY

In a sad turn of events in what seemed to happen in the blink of an eye, Ivy was orphaned when both of her parents died in a car accident.

"Gunner, something terrible has happened. Your aunt Louise and uncle Brian died yesterday."

"What happened, mom?" asked Gunner.

"The police called and said they died in a head-on car crash last night."

"How could this have happened?" said a tearful Gunner, unsure how to make sense of the worst news he'd ever heard in his life. "You mean I'll never see them again?"

"The police said the other driver was speeding and lost control of his car. The other driver died too. There was nothing the doctors could do to save them. I'm so sorry, Gunner. They're in Heaven now," said Charlotte, fighting back her tears, trying to stay strong while hugging Gunner.

"Where's Ivy? I have to talk to her," said Gunner while wiping the tears as they streamed down his face.

"The children's service for the County has taken her in for the time being. She's in a children's home. Soon they'll place her with a foster family. Foster families take children in and care for them until they're adopted by their permanent families."

"You mean I won't see Ivy again either?"

"We'll see Ivy as much as possible, Gunner. We're not sure what's going to happen to her or where she'll live. Everything is happening so fast."

"No! No! I want to see Ivy today. Take me to Ivy now." Gunner cried at the thought that Ivy could be left all alone, and he was determined to help her. Suddenly, the perfect solution occurred to Gunner.

"Mom, why don't we ask Ivy to live with us?" He pleaded. "She's my best friend. What if she moves away and I never see her again? Ivy always listens to me. She plays games with me. She makes me laugh. Mom, why can't we go get her now and bring her to our house?"

Charlotte loved Ivy, and she knew Donovan loved Ivy, too. "Gunner, that's a great idea."

"Why don't we adopt her? Why can't we be her permanent family?"

"Gunner, if we officially adopt Ivy, it isn't automatic. We'll have to go through the County's process to make it permanent. I'll talk with your father as soon as he gets home."

"I'll talk to him, too. I know he'll say yes when I tell him Ivy needs us."

Charlotte and Donovan contacted the County about adoption and learned that since Ivy was Charlotte's niece, the Coles' adoption request would be considered an urgent matter. But first, there would be an interview process, paperwork to complete, and a home visit. Donovan and Charlotte were also required to attend a ten-week course which they eagerly agreed to complete.

Gunner, Charlotte and Donovan visited Ivy at her foster home where she'd just been placed. While sitting on their back porch, Charlotte and Donovan extended their invitation to Ivy. "Ivy, how would you like to live with Gunner and us? We all talked about it, and we'd like you to be a part of our family permanently. I'll be your mom and Donovan can be your dad. Would you like that?"

"It was my idea, Ivy. If we live together, we can play all we want. Please say yes," said Gunner, grinning ear-to-ear and bouncing up and down so much that his parents could hardly contain him.

Ivy couldn't believe her ears. She cried with excitement and breathed a huge sigh of relief. Ivy had been feeling frightened. She was tearful and had been struggling with sleep since the tragic event. The new family were strangers to her, and Ivy had no idea where her permanent home was going to be. No one had given her any reassurance about what was going to happen to her. "Thank you, thank you." Ivy hugged Charlotte and her new dad for the longest time, then wiped her tears away with the back of her small hand. She knew she'd found her pot of gold at the end of the rainbow.

"I contacted the children's service. Donovan and I have to complete a ten- week course before we can officially adopt you. But I'm sure there won't be any problems."

"You mean I have to wait ten weeks?"

"Ivy, the children's service said that you could move in before that. You can move into our house as soon as next week."

"Ivy, we'll take care of you forever. You'll be my sister-cousin. Won't that be fun?" said Gunner.

"I'll tell my foster parents. I'm sure they'll be happy for me."

Nine days later, the Cole's returned to Ivy's foster home to welcome her into their lives. Waving good-bye to her foster family, Ivy jumped into the back seat of the Cole's family car. Charlotte and Donovan were sure that Ivy would be excited once she saw their welcome home surprise waiting for her.

The moment Ivy stepped into her new home, Audie welcomed Ivy, showering her with his usual doses of licking. Audie jumped on the family's well-worn, perfect-for-the-dog sofa as if to corner a seated Ivy to inform her of the rules of the house.

He's the king, and each member of the household was required to treat him as such. Ivy quickly got the message, and soon the two of them were inseparable.

As part of Ivy's welcome to her new home, Charlotte and Donovan decided to spruce up Ivy's bedroom to make it her own special room. The Cole's decided to paint Ivy's room pink, her favorite color and the color of her favorite candy, pink taffy.

"Ivy," said an excited Gunner, "We have a surprise for you. Close your eyes, I wanna show you your new room. Take my arm and keep your eyes closed until I tell you to open them."

Ivy smiled the instant she opened her eyes. She'd forgotten that she once had told Gunner that pink was her favorite color. Ivy's twin bed had a white and pink bedspread with pink roses and dahlias, lifelike green stems, and a four-inch-wide eyelet ruffle around the entire spread. Ivy thought the flowers looked so lifelike that she imagined she could pick the flowers to smell their perfumed fragrance. Ivy's new bed also had two ginormous pillows. They were so inviting that Ivy couldn't resist jumping into their softness as soon as she saw them.

"Ivy, we hope you like your new room. Everything is new. Gunner helped pick out the furniture."

"I helped paint too, Ivy. And I picked out your favorite books."

"It's beautiful! You mean everything is all mine?"

"Yes, Ivy. You have your own corner desk, two dressers, with bookcases on top of each dresser. And here's the books Gunner picked out."

"My favorite books! *Hannah Saves the Word* and *Wish*!" Ivy couldn't help but imagine lying on her stomach every night reading her books in bed.

***

Ivy was elated to be with her new family and enjoyed her routine of homework, followed by dinner, and her special time with Audie.

One evening, several months after settling into her new life and just after her tenth birthday, Ivy noticed that she felt queasy. She also felt light-headed and had an upset stomach. Ivy had no idea what was going on with her. She was uncomfortable and restless. Gunner and Audie, who were nearby, noticed a change in Ivy as well.

Without any special training, Audie seemed to know instinctively what to do. He nervously pushed his nose on Ivy's right calf, as if to alert Ivy that something was indeed wrong. In an instant, Ivy dropped her pencil and had an absent look about her. She didn't respond when Gunner asked her what was wrong. Gunner watched in fear as Ivy appeared to get sicker and sicker. Ivy began rubbing her right hand and she began smacking her lips.

"Mom, help! Something's wrong with Ivy. Audie barked at her and Ivy didn't even look at her."

Charlotte was by Ivy's side in seconds. After a brief time, Ivy snapped out of her trance and soon recognized her adoptive mom, Gunner, and Audie.

"Ivy, are you alright? Can you tell me what happened?"

"I felt jiggly. I forgot where I was and I couldn't move."

"Well, I'm sure you'll be fine," Charlotte said reassuringly, "but I think we should talk to a doctor first thing tomorrow."

***

"Dr. Grant, my husband and I adopted Ivy several months ago after both of her parents died. Ivy's mother was my sister. Ivy is my niece. Last night, around seven o'clock, my son, Gunner, told me something was wrong with Ivy. Gunner said her name, but Ivy couldn't respond. She was rubbing her hands and smacking her lips. The next minute, she was alert again, and appeared to be fine."

"Dr. Grant, what happened to me?" asked Ivy.

"Have you fallen or hurt your head recently, Ivy?" Dr. Grant asked, while looking at Ivy's ears, nose and eyes.

"No, Doctor."

"How long ago did your parents die?"

"My parents died on March 18th."

"That must have been very traumatic for you. Were you their only child?"

"Yes, Doctor, I was home with my babysitter at the time. A police car drove up our driveway, and three people jumped out and rushed to the front door. I was really scared. They knocked on the door. My babysitter let them in, and a lady in a dark blue suit took my arm and told me my parents had just been killed in a car accident. I cried myself to sleep. Once my aunt and uncle officially adopted me, they said I could call them mom and dad. I love that. Before I moved in with them, I lived in a place called a foster home."

"What else do you recall about what happened to you last night? Can you tell me how long your episode lasted?"

"No, Doctor Grant. I can only remember feeling jiggly. I didn't understand what was going on around me, my stomach hurt, and afterwards I felt sleepy."

"Did your arms and legs twitch or shake?"

"I don't think so. I know what you mean, though, because that used to happen to my birth mom before she died. She had seizures that she had to take medicine for."

"Did she tell you that she had a condition called epilepsy?"

"Yes, Doctor, that's what my mom had. She's had seizures ever since I can remember. Sometimes I watched her to help keep her safe. Other times my dad took her to the hospital."

"Ivy, you may have the same condition as your mother. By any chance, do you know how old she was when she had her first seizure?"

"My sister had her first seizure when she was eighteen, Dr. Grant."

"Thanks, Charlotte. That's helpful." While scratching his thick gray beard and taking notes, Dr. Grant collected more information as he considered how best to help Ivy.

Ivy waited patiently and thought about how lucky she was to be in Dr. Grant's office. Ivy thought that he had a friendly smile and a calm expression framed by his squared spectacles that assured her that everything was going to be okay.

While sitting in Dr. Grant's office, Charlotte and Ivy studied every decorative artifact he had on display. Near his desk was his medical degree from the University of North Carolina with his name on it. The room itself, a soft light gray, was full of a number of curious objects. A tall medicine cabinet was jammed with what Ivy imagined to be full of all sorts of medications, band-aids, and maybe even secret concoctions of cures for his patients. She scrutinized his emergency kit and couldn't help but wonder what kinds of emergencies took place in his office. Ivy also noticed a glass screen that she'd assumed was used to look at x-rays, and she wondered if a picture of her brain would be posted there for her to look at. As Ivy turned her attention back to Dr. Grant in his long white coat and stethoscope draped around his neck, she'd hoped Dr. Grant could promise her that nothing was wrong with her.

Turning to both Ivy and Charlotte, Dr. Grant said, "It's very possible that Ivy had a seizure last night, but I can't be sure. I don't see the need for medication just yet. But if another episode like this happens, it's critical that I see you again."

"Is this serious, Dr. Grant?" a worried Charlotte asked.

"There's no need to diagnose Ivy with epilepsy yet, Mrs. Cole. But Ivy, if you begin to feel the same symptoms again, you must tell us. Will you promise me that? There are many different types of seizures. With some you stare, and with other seizures the whole body might shake. Some last only a few seconds, and other times the seizure can last much longer."

"Yes, Doctor, I promise."

"I'd like to do some routine bloodwork today, just to make sure there's nothing that shows up out of the ordinary."

While walking with Ivy to the car, Charlotte was curious about how much Ivy knew about her mother's epilepsy. "Ivy, how often did your mom have seizures?"

"Well, I think I worried about mom having seizures more than how often she actually had them. Maybe a couple of times a year. But I worried about her all the time."

"I remember your mom having grand mal seizures, but I guess I really don't know how often they were. I recall that her doctor tried her on a number of different medications. Your mom was always brave. She had a positive attitude about her life, and she refused to ever let her epilepsy get her down."

"Dad said she had convulsions and that's why she went to the hospital," said Ivy.

"Your mom started having grand mal seizures when she was around eighteen, Ivy. The first time really worried us. We'd never seen anything like it and didn't know what could have caused it. Your mom had two grand mal seizures within one week. After that, she was diagnosed with epilepsy and put on medication. Her arms and legs shook. After she recovered from her seizure, she had no memory of what had happened."

"Do you know what caused my mom's seizures?"

"Her doctors never found the actual cause. Your mom decided to cope with it the best she could. Fear of having another seizure never really slowed her down, though. She went on to college, had fun with her friends, and then fell in love with your dad. They got married after a year of dating. Then she became pregnant with you."

What is Epilepsy?

Epilepsy is a seizure disorder. A person who has two or more unprovoked seizures (seizures caused by abnormal brain signals) is thought to have epilepsy. Often the cause of the seizure cannot be identified easily. Medication usually is needed to control the seizures.

Medical scientists continue to research the cause of epilepsy. Scientists do know that epilepsy is associated with abnormalities in brain chemistry. These abnormalities interfere with how brain cells send signals to each other. Also, epilepsy tends to run in families, meaning it can be inherited.

The butterfly symbolizes freedom and hope for those with epilepsy.

Additional Information

Lennox-Gastaut syndrome: Lennox-Gastaut syndrome (LGS) is a type of epilepsy. Patients with LGS experience many different types of seizures including: Tonic - stiffening of the body; Atonic - temporary loss of muscle tone and consciousness, causing the patient to fall; Atypical absence - staring episodes.

Dravet syndrome: Dravet syndrome is a rare, drug-resistant epilepsy that begins in the first year of life in an otherwise healthy infant. It is lifelong. It usually presents with a prolonged seizure with fever that affects one side of the body. Most cases are due to severe SCN1A gene mutations.

***

Ivy put the events of that frightening evening behind her and continued to adjust happily to her new life. She loved her special time with Audie. Gunner told Ivy how much Audie had taught him about life. "Audie taught me to be kind, he taught me how to ask for attention, and he knows it's important to do homework and brush her teeth. Dad and I brush our teeth every night before we go to bed. Then Dad brushes Audie's teeth. Audie loves this special time with us. Ivy, you know what? Audie knows everything."

"You don't have to tell me that, Gunner. Audie knew something was wrong when I felt funny. He's the smartest dog I've ever known."

Several months later, in a flash of what seemed to come out of the blue, Ivy felt that same funny feeling again. Ivy knew she'd promised the doctor and her mom that she would tell them if she felt poorly. Just as before, Audie jumped to Ivy's side in a sudden single leap. After pushing Ivy's calf with his nose, he also yelped a special anxious bark.

"Mom, it's happening again. Help."

Charlotte, Donovan, Gunner and Audie stayed by her side. Ivy was unresponsive and disoriented. And just as before, she was rubbing her hands and smacking her lips. Audie sat on her leg, waiting patiently for his new best friend to respond.

This time, Charlotte timed Ivy's episode and within a few minutes, Ivy was alert and saw four pairs of eyes peering back at her with love and concern. "Was I staring off again?" said Ivy.

"Ivy, do you remember anything? Do you remember your name being called?"

"I could sense that you were here with me, but I just couldn't respond."

"I'll to get an appointment with Dr. Grant tomorrow," Charlotte said.

> Most seizures happen suddenly without warning, last a short time (a few seconds or minutes), and stop by themselves.

Ivy's First Aid Plan for Complex Partial Seizure

- Stay with Ivy until her seizure ends and she is fully alert. After it ends, make sure she sits in a safe place.
- Once she is alert and able to communicate, tell her what happened in very simple terms.
- Comfort Ivy and speak calmly.
- Check her medical bracelet or other emergency information.
- Keep yourself and other people calm.

How to Assist Someone with a Grand Mal Seizure

- Ease him/her to the floor.
- Turn him/her gently onto one side. This will help him/her breathe.
- Clear the area near him/her of anything hard or sharp. This can prevent injury.
- Put something soft and flat, like a folded jacket, under his/her head.
- Remove eyeglasses.
- Loosen ties or anything around his/her neck that may make it hard to breathe.
- Time the seizure. Call 911 if the seizure lasts longer than 5 minutes.

Never do any of the Following during a Seizure

- Do **not** hold the person down or try to stop their movements.
- Do **not** put anything in their mouth. This can injure teeth or jaw. A person having a seizure cannot swallow his or her tongue.
- Do **not** try to give mouth-to-mouth breaths (like CPR). People usually start breathing again on their own after a seizure.
- Do **not** offer the person water or food until they are fully alert.

***

The following day, Ivy sat patiently in Dr. Grant's office. "Ivy, your mother thinks you've had a seizure. Is that correct?"

"Yes, Dr. Grant."

"Can you describe your symptoms to me? Did you know what was going on around you while this was happening?"

"I don't think so. Mom said she thought I was twitching a little."

"She was also rubbing her hands some, her lips were smacking, and her arm moved funny. It didn't last more than a few minutes," added Charlotte.

"And Ivy had trouble remembering what had occurred? Did she appear confused?"

"That's right," both responded, nodding their heads in agreement.

"Well, it's possible Ivy had a seizure, just as you suspected." Turning to Charlotte, Dr. Grant said with reassurance, "You did the right thing by bringing Ivy in to see me. I'd like to run some additional tests to assess Ivy's overall health. The tests might signal a chemical imbalance that could be the cause of her seizures. Ivy, I'd like to complete these tests today. Would that be alright?"

"Sure, Doctor Grant, I want to know what caused my seizure."

"Well, I can't guarantee that we'll ever know the cause of your seizures. Sixty percent of my patients never find out the cause of their seizures. I'd also like to do an EEG today. That's short for electroencephalogram. The test records the electrical activity in your brain. It'll help me determine the type of seizure you've had and where in your brain the seizure began."

Ivy's eyes grew big. "Will the test hurt? How can you look at my brain?"

"Don't worry, Ivy, the test won't hurt, and you'll know what's going on the entire time. My nurse will come in and attach tiny electrodes to your scalp that have small metal discs. The electrodes detect tiny electrical charges that result from the activity of your brain cells. I'll come in and monitor your brain activity. I'll have the results right away so I can share them with you and your mother.

"Dr. Grant, will Ivy need medication?" asked Charlotte.

"Well, first I'd like to review the test results from her EEG and bloodwork, but I'm guessing I'll need to call a prescription in to the pharmacy. Once someone experiences two unprovoked seizures, they're generally considered to have the diagnosis of epilepsy."

Turning to Ivy, Dr. Grant said, "Ivy, do you have any questions before we begin?"

Barely able to take in the news of her diagnosis, all that Ivy heard was the 'E' word. *What does that mean? Will I live with this forever?* "Dr. Grant, I hope you can help me."

"I'm confident I can help you, Ivy. According to the symptoms you've experienced, it sounds like you have the type of epilepsy we call complex partial seizures. We'll have to monitor this over time, but there are medications that can help control your seizures."

***

Ivy sat patiently while a friendly nurse attached the electrodes to her scalp. "Dr. Grant was right," Ivy smiled, "This doesn't hurt at all!"

Jenna, Dr. Grant's nurse, was a very cheerful person. Ivy thought she was fun, too, because she laughed and was friendly. "This test is pain free, Ivy. We do these all the time in our office. It helps Dr. Grant do his job."

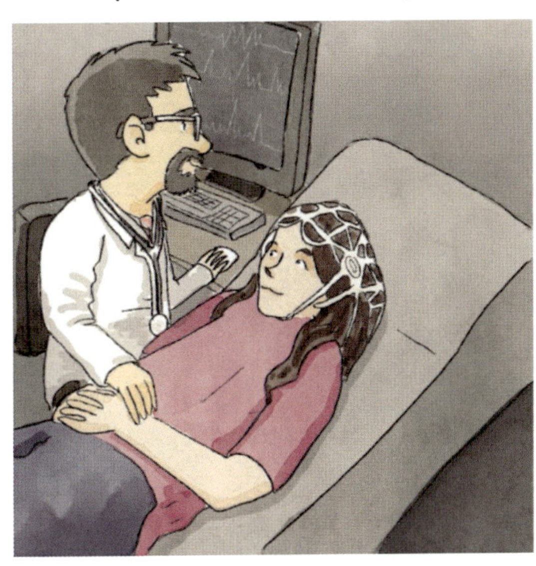

Following a review of the tests, Dr. Grant informed Ivy and Charlotte that he'd spotted a slight abnormality on Ivy's EEG. He confirmed Ivy's diagnosis of epilepsy after asking additional questions and verifying once again that there'd been no recent head injuries, infections, or other illnesses.

"Ivy, I'd like to tell you a little bit more about epilepsy. Cells in your brain make everything in your body work by sending electrical signals to each other. When a seizure happens, a sudden change occurs in how the brain's cells send signals to each other. And when this happens, you begin to feel funny."

"Like tingly, jiggly, and not remembering?"

"Yes, that's correct. I hope the medication I'm prescribing will eliminate your seizures completely. The name of it is Carbamazepine. I'll start you off on a low dose so you shouldn't notice any side effects. All medications could have some side effects, though, so if you notice any unpleasant changes, I want you to call my nurse."

"What are some of the side effects Ivy should be keeping an eye out for, Dr. Grant?" inquired Charlotte.

"Call me if Ivy complains of a sore throat, rash, fever, nosebleeds or serious skin reactions. I'll send you home with a list of everything to watch out for. I also recommend that you stay out of direct sunlight and wear protective clothing. You should also remember to wear sunglasses. Put on sunscreen with at least an SPF of 15. It'll all be clearly stated in the handout I'm giving you."

Charlotte drove to the pharmacy while a quiet Ivy sat next to her in the front seat. "Mom, do you think my new medication will cure me? What's it called again?"

"Dr. Grant hopes this medication is all you need. In fact, he's prescribed only a small dose, so I doubt you'll have any side effects. As a matter of fact, I'm relieved that we saw Dr. Grant today. He's given us a diagnosis and a solution. The name of your medication is called Carbamazepine. Did you know that Dr. Grant specializes in the treatment of children with epilepsy? We're really lucky he could see you today."

"I want to take my medication as soon as I can."

"Let's wait for dinner, honey. Remember, Dr. Grant told you to take this medicine with food. It might help to avoid any stomach upset."

***

Audie jumped for joy as soon as Ivy walked through the door. Audie stayed by her side as if to tell her she could always count on him. Ivy, too, was so happy to see

Audie after such a long time at the doctor's office that she'd planned to play with him for the rest of the night. She didn't want to do her homework; she only wanted to smother Audie with love.

Ivy's mother smiled with relief and thought to herself, *I wonder who's rescuing who?* Audie, after all, had exhibited anxiety and had known that another seizure was about to occur. How did he know? Was Audie born with this special talent?

At dinner, Charlotte shared her new idea with Ivy. "Ivy, how would you like it if Audie slept in bed with you from now on? He seems to want to take care of you, so why don't we let him?"

"I'd love that," Ivy said, "This is like having Christmas early! Audie, come here boy, you wanna be my sleeping buddy?"

"Ivy, did you know there are special dogs called alert dogs? They can detect when a seizure might be coming, and they alert their owner."

"You mean, Audie might be my very own alert dog?"

"Ivy, all of us noticed that somehow Audie knew you were about to have a seizure before it began. I think we should ask Dr. Grant if he's ever heard of such a thing."

"Maybe we could even bring Audie along to my next appointment."

"For now, let's leave him home. Let's just ask Dr. Grant if it's really possible whether some dogs have this special talent.

***

At Ivy's follow-up visit, Dr. Grant said to Charlotte and Ivy, "Today we'll talk about individual steps you have to take and how we will use a team approach in managing your epilepsy. Ivy, the most important thing you can do for now is to take your medications, continue to see me, and follow my recommendations."

"Like what, Doctor?"

"First of all, it's important that you follow a routine sleep schedule, eat well, and exercise.

"Dr. Grant, what can I do to help Ivy?" Charlotte said.

"For now, I think Ivy should begin keeping a seizure diary."

Dr. Grant turned to Ivy and said, "Your diary will be about your seizures, of course, but you can also record your moods, write down any side effects from your meds, any stress you feel, exercise that you do, and how healthy you're eating. I also think you might benefit from wearing a special bracelet. It'll have your diagnosis, medication information, and telephone number on it."

"Where can I get one?" asked Charlotte.

"A lot of major retailers sell them on the Internet. Ivy, has your medication caused you any problems over the past month?"

"No, Doctor. I haven't had any stomach aches. I haven't even felt tired, and I haven't had any rashes."

"That's good news, indeed. I'm hopeful that this medication is the right medication for you, Ivy. I think you'll find that keeping a diary is going to be fun. And if you have another seizure, your diary could help me manage your epilepsy better."

"What other things should I do, Dr. Grant?"

"For starters, Ivy, try to get around nine to ten hours of sleep each night. Most pre-teens and teens don't sleep enough, and that isn't good for them. If you, Ivy, don't get enough sleep, it could put you at risk for having another seizure."

"What about Ivy's nutrition, Dr. Grant?" asked Charlotte.

"I'd like Ivy to eat plenty of fruits, vegetables, nuts, seeds, and beans. Skip candy bars or any extra sugar. I use this eating plan with all of my patients. Here at the clinic, we believe eating healthy is a preventive measure to avoid most diseases. You're lucky you're only ten, Ivy. If you learn to eat healthy now, you'll have a head start compared to everyone else in the whole country."

"Does the clinic have any brochures or books about epilepsy that we can take home?" asked Charlotte.

"I'll have my nurse give you our information about first aid, a sample diary, and a guide to healthy eating. I'd also like to do more blood work today. With Carbamazepine we'll need to check what's called a blood level every few months. The medication in your blood level needs to remain within a certain range. In particular, if it's too low, I'll need to increase the dosage."

"Ick." Ivy's go-to word at the thought of more needles. Ivy couldn't hide her scrunched expression, but she needed to be brave. "Okay, Doctor."

"I'll call you tomorrow with the results, Mrs. Cole. I'll also send you home with a list of Internet links that'll provide you with more information about epilepsy."

Charlotte then said, "Before we leave, Doctor, I want to mention two things. First, I've spoken at length with Ivy's teacher and the school's nurse. They told me that there are other students at her school with epilepsy. I'm feeling encouraged that the school staff are well prepared if Ivy has a seizure. Second, we wanted to talk about our dog Audie."

"What about your dog?" asked Dr. Grant.

"Dr. Grant, I think my dog knew when I was going to have a seizure even before I could tell. He put his nose on my calf and smelled and nudged me, and then he barked. Mom said he might be what's called an alert dog."

Scratching his head while donning a half-frown, Dr. Grant seemed uncertain as to how to respond to his young patient who was clearly beaming with excitement. "To tell you the truth, I have a few patients who rely on their dogs to alert them. Some dogs seem to know instinctively. I have other patients who have several seizures a week, and they need a dog with special training that can provide a service to them after they've had a seizure. These dogs help my adult patients live more independently."

"Dr. Grant, Audie hasn't had any training, but I've read that there are several agencies that train service dogs to help patients with epilepsy," Charlotte said.

"There's a difference between service dogs and alert dogs. Alert dogs are believed to sense an oncoming seizure. Most believe it's because of the dog's exceptional sense of smell. A service dog, on the other hand, can be trained to do anything you need them to do once the seizure has begun."

"Doctor, you mean Audie is special?" Ivy said in her typical excited and hopeful voice.

"I'm glad your dog helped. It sounds like you have a special bond with him. You say Audie actually jumped to you and gave you a nudge just before your seizure?"

"Yes, Dr. Grant, both times."

"Well, then, perhaps we'll include Audie as a member of your healthcare team. However, the definition of a true service dog requires one to two years of training, so Audie cannot be considered an official service dog. That means he can't go with you to school. But the good news so far is that you don't need this kind of special assistance."

"So, you believe we should not look into service dogs for now?" Charlotte clarified.

"That's right. Obtaining a service dog requires a big commitment. They also cost over twenty thousand dollars."

> Epilepsy affects over three million Americans each year, making it more common than cerebral palsy, multiple sclerosis, muscular dystrophy, and Parkinson's disease combined.

> You can't catch epilepsy from another person. Anyone can develop epilepsy. Seizures start in people over age 65 almost as often as it does in children.

Ivy's Health Care Team

☺ Most important, is that Ivy practice healthy self-care steps such as getting plenty of rest, exercise and good nutrition.

🕐 Ivy must take her medications on time. Ivy can ask her family to remind her. She can use a pill box; and she can also set up a reminder on her cell phone.

☞ Ivy must inform her teacher(s) about her condition. Her teacher(s) can provide reassurance that they know how to help her. They can also give her any added attention she may need, such as attending to her mood and giving her suggestions about how to cope with epilepsy. Other classmates who also have epilepsy can be her support system.

✍ Ivy can begin to take charge of her own care by keeping a daily diary about her mood (just using emoji's), taking her pills, exercise, sleep and nutrition.

💻 Ivy and her family can research the Internet, set up her own personalized folder of information that are important to teens with epilepsy. Ivy can challenge herself by making up her own puzzles and sharing with others.

🕯 Ivy must be careful to never burn the candle at both ends. Added stress has the potential to trigger a seizure.

👓 Rely on her medical doctor and listen to his/her recommendations. Sharing her diary will help them at each of her follow up visits.

Call the nursing staff with any concerns.

Get extra help by talking to a dietitian.

Recognize and trust Audie's instinct to alert her of an impending seizure.

Sleep and Epilepsy

- How much sleep is enough? Age 5 – 12; 10-11 hours of sleep; Teens 8 ½ - 9 ½
- More than 50% of teens report daytime sleepiness
- Teens who feel unhappy/tense and drink two or more caffeinated beverages per day are more likely to sleep less and feel sleepy during the day
- Teens who get optimal sleep are more likely to achieve A's and B's
- Insufficient sleep nights increase with the number of bedroom electronics
- Sleep deprivation increases risk of seizures and epileptic discharges on EEG
- Conditions that lead to sleep fragmentation, including seizures and sleep disorders pose further risk for seizures
- Daytime sleepiness is the most common complaint of people with epilepsy and impairs quality of life
- Extreme sleep deprivation can cause seizures in people with epilepsy and people without epilepsy
- Minor amounts of sleep loss can provoke seizures in some people with epilepsy
- People with focal seizures who sleep 6 hours or less on average have more frequent seizures than those who sleep longer
- Tips for a good night's sleep:
    - Think positive
    - Establish fixed bed and wake times
    - Relax before going to bed
    - Maintain a comfortable sleeping environment
    - Avoid clock watching
    - Use the bedroom for sleep only
    - Avoid daytime naps
    - Avoid caffeine, alcohol, nicotine
    - Avoid strenuous activities within 3 hours of bedtime.

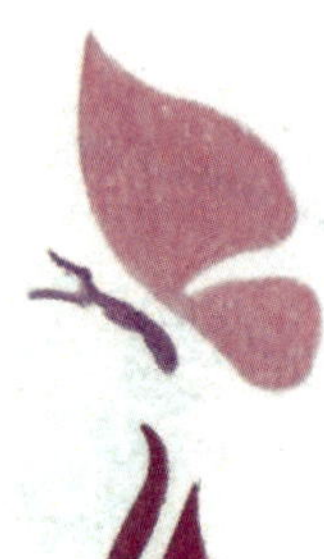

***

The following day, Ivy curled up with Audie on the couch to read the information she'd gotten from Dr. Grant. Ivy was eager to begin writing in her new diary.

"Mom, will you help me with my diary?"

"Ivy, I've been reading the pamphlets that Dr. Grant gave us about keeping a diary. While you were at school today, I drew up a chart." Sitting down beside Ivy, Charlotte showed Ivy the design she'd come up with. "I listed some symptoms and boxes to check, in order to make it quick and easy for you. Each page covers one week."

"Can you help me with my diet too?"

"Of course. We're all going to eat better, Ivy. We're all in this together."

"Should I write about Audie, too?"

"Yep, I added a special box just for Audie and how he helps. Watch Audie closely, and see how he acts around you. If he smells your calf or nudges you, I want you to tell me immediately, ok?"

> Some people have more than one type of seizure, or their seizures may not fit clearly into the typical classifications of seizure types. But even if someone's seizures are unique, they usually follow the same pattern each time they happen.

> Is swimming with epilepsy allowed? The International League Against Epilepsy (ILAE) has published guidelines which say that swimming is permitted for people with epilepsy at their neurologist's discretion. This means that if you have epilepsy and would like to go swimming, you should ask your doctor first.

IVY'S SEIZURE DIARY

	Sunday	Monday	Tuesday	Wednesday	Thursday	Friday	Saturday
Mood							
Notes							
Seizure:							
Tingly							
Hard to respond							
Loss of Awareness							
Smells							
Lip Smack							
Limb movement							
Triggers?							
Nausea							
Other							
Time							
Length							
Date							
Location							
Dr. Visit							
Meds							
Side Effect							
What did Audie do?							
School							
Sleep							
Exercise							
Food							

Emoji Key for Mood:           

Audie knew they were talking about him. Audie's ears perked up and his tail wagged, so Ivy gave him an extra tight hug and his favorite kibble treat. "Mom, look, Audie's smiling at us."

"Audie knows he's the top dog in this house."

"Mom, what do you think I could train Audie to do if I have another seizure?"

"I read that some owners train their dogs to fetch medicine. For now, I think it's important that we train him to stay by your side and bark and give you his special nudges. We could train Audie to come to me and bark, too. I also called the vet today, and there's a trainer who lives near us. Her name is Olivia and we can make an appointment with her in the next month or two."

"This is so exciting. Audie will have his own special job!"

"I know you like puzzles, and I thought you and I could make up our own puzzles in addition to keeping a diary. The puzzles could contain words about epilepsy, nutrition, and even about seizure alert dogs."

"Like a crossword puzzle?"

"Yes, Ivy, and we could add a word search puzzle, too. Wouldn't that be fun?"

Words Related to Epilepsy

J	G	B	R	Q	G	N	I	H	C	T	I	W	T	C	Y	A	S	O	O
Z	D	I	A	T	S	R	I	F	S	T	R	E	S	S	C	B	M	S	M
V	L	Q	U	R	T	Q	H	U	M	C	J	G	L	B	A	S	G	V	K
B	A	Z	B	E	W	V	L	R	F	C	A	K	Q	V	D	E	E	K	R
B	C	A	Y	S	K	Y	I	R	E	A	R	U	A	C	I	N	O	L	C
M	O	Y	W	Q	I	M	E	D	I	C	A	T	I	O	N	C	R	H	E
J	F	Y	R	O	M	E	M	G	M	O	D	I	E	T	D	E	J	C	X
Z	T	L	G	B	C	J	Y	R	E	G	R	U	S	E	H	P	O	S	D
M	L	Y	O	P	E	E	L	S	S	M	R	S	T	R	G	N	F	Y	S
B	V	F	D	H	E	A	R	T	T	E	E	N	S	S	V	Y	A	E	D
I	D	F	E	S	G	N	I	H	T	A	E	R	B	U	P	H	L	D	S
C	E	C	C	T	E	C	V	E	V	G	F	S	L	V	T	G	L	K	V
W	R	O	I	D	V	D	A	J	P	U	R	S	A	O	G	Z	I	M	E
B	A	N	V	O	X	V	E	U	M	I	I	G	N	I	J	Y	N	R	H
H	C	F	R	N	U	L	B	K	S	O	L	I	W	Q	T	X	G	Y	C
C	S	U	E	X	R	J	N	W	N	E	C	E	D	I	A	R	Y	X	A
L	E	S	S	W	Y	A	D	S	P	H	S	J	P	H	E	L	P	Y	D
I	A	I	Y	S	E	M	O	C	T	U	O	U	C	S	W	J	B	Z	A
J	X	O	T	G	N	I	R	A	T	S	A	K	E	Z	Y	R	U	V	E
Y	L	N	G	B	C	Z	Y	V	T	R	I	G	G	E	R	S	I	M	H

Word List

ABSENCE
AURA
BREATHING
CAUSES
CLONIC
CONFUSION
CONVULSIONS
DIARY

DIET
EPILEPSY
FALLING
FIRSTAID
FOCAL
HEADACHE
HEART
HELP

IVY
MEDICATION
MEMORY
OUTCOMES
SCARED
SERVICEDOG
SLEEP
STARING

STRESS
SURGERY
TEENS
TONIC
TRIGGERS
TWITCHING
WIGGLES

***

Over the next several months, Ivy learned a lot about epilepsy. She enjoyed keeping her diary, she learned about the different types of seizures, especially complex partial seizures, and the diary helped her pay attention to her daily moods.

At home, Ivy and Gunner enjoyed playing Scrabble together which was Ivy's favorite. Gunner preferred a game called Sorry because he won that game more often. Lately, though, he'd become mesmerized by the shoot'em-up games on his computer. Ivy didn't like these games as much. The fast moves and the flashing lights on the screen made her feel uncomfortable. Ivy instead enjoyed hours of play throwing the ball in the back yard with Audie. Other times, she put Audie's leash on him, and they visited the other dogs in the neighborhood. This gave Audie time for socializing and rolling around with his favorite furry friends.

Many months had passed since her second seizure, and Ivy and Dr. Grant were relieved that her seizures were controlled by her medication.

***

Just before the holidays, Audie's new trainer, Olivia, came to the Cole home for her first visit to meet Audie and begin his training. Olivia was an energetic and friendly college student with a twinkle in her deep brown eyes. She kept her long dark brown hair tied in a pony tail with a green sparkly scrunchie. After Audie gave Olivia the once over with a few sniffs, Audie decided Olivia could stay. "Ivy, I'd like to give Audie a treat. Is that alright with you?"

"Sure, Olivia, whatever you think is best."

"I'm checking to see if food is the best way to train Audie."

Ivy clapped as she witnessed Audie dance for the kibble Olivia showed him. It was liver flavored. "Audie likes your treat more than the ones I give him."

"Ivy, the most important thing in training your dog is to have a trusting relationship. Your goal is to develop a solid bond with him."

"I'm sure Audie trusts me. I play with him every day, he sleeps in my bed, and he wants to lick my face all the time."

"Do you tease him? Do you let others grab him or tease him?"

"No, never. Audie doesn't like teasing."

"Good. It's also critical that you figure out the best way to tell your friends whether or not you'll allow them to pet him."

"What do you mean? What should I say?"

"First of all, if Audie doesn't want to meet someone, trust his instincts and don't make him. Practice what to tell your friends about whether or not they can approach him. He's your alert dog, and this is his main purpose, so he can't jump around and play with your friends. He must understand that he is required to stay by your side, and your friends must understand this, too. No ifs, ands, or buts about it. I was glad to learn that there were no other dogs in the house."

"How do I train him to stay by my side?"

"If he likes food, we'll use food as his reward. Each time he comes when you call him, he gets a treat. Then you'll want to reward him a second time for staying by your side. Tell me about how Audie alerted you that you were about to have a seizure."

"Olivia, he just knew. He pushed on my right calf, right here," as Ivy pointed to a spot on her right, mid-calf, "He wouldn't stop, he just kept pushing. I could tell he was trying to warn me. He was trying to get my attention."

"Did he do anything else?"

"Then he barked at me. I noticed, but when I start to have a seizure, I'm slow to respond. I just freeze."

"Anything else?"

"He stays by my side."

"That's a wonderful story, Ivy. Some dogs, and it sounds like Audie is one of them, have a super keen sense of smell. Today, we'll practice how to train Audie to come every time you call him. Then I'll demonstrate how to train him to sit next to you. You have to be the leader. If you're not, then Audie might get anxious, or decide he's the leader, and we don't want that. Ivy, caring for Audie will require a big commitment from you."

"I think I can do this. I want to train him the best way I can."

"Okay, but because you're only ten, I'd like your mom to be involved too."

"I was thinking the same thing," Charlotte said. "I spent a lot of time with Audie before Ivy moved in with us. And when Ivy goes off to college, I expect I'll be Audie's main companion again. I'm a stay-at-home mom, so I spend the day with Audie until the kids come home from school. Ivy's neurologist thinks it's much too soon to conclude that Ivy needs a real service dog. Ivy's medications are doing their job."

"I agree. Also, alert dogs, in my experience, work best with owners who have grand mal seizures and those owners who have seizures at least once a month. The reason being is that the owner must be visibly distressed."

"Ivy has only had two seizures. We could all tell by looking at Ivy that something was wrong, but they weren't grand mal seizures."

"Well, that's good news for Ivy. For now, it sounds like Audie won't require training to be an official service dog. I can still teach you and Ivy important training principles that'll help Ivy and Audie develop a closer bond. Audie doesn't need to be trained as an alert dog because you're convinced that Audie possesses this innate skill already, correct?"

"We've all witnessed it, Olivia. On both occasions."

"Okay, then, I think the important goals for today are to teach you how to train Audie through positive reinforcement. Consistency is the most important principle to master in dog training. Do you think Audie is a very dominant dog?"

"Not really, he usually wants to please us."

"The reason I'm asking is, if Audie becomes aggressive at all in this process, he would not be considered a good candidate to be a true service dog, should you ever need one."

"Good to know, Olivia. I also heard what you said to Ivy about what to tell her friends. She'll need help with this."

"Ivy, you'll need to decide if you want friends or strangers to pet him."

"I think it would be easier to tell strangers not to pet him. But I'd like my friends who come to my house to be able to pet him when I tell Audie it's okay."

"Let's rehearse what you can say to strangers while you're walking Audie. How about, 'My dog is a working dog, please do not pet him.'"

"I'll explain that Audie is getting special training."

"That's good, Ivy. Most people, once it's explained to them, are happy to cooperate."

***

After Christmas break, Ivy saw Dr. Grant for one of her routine appointments to get her blood level tested. "Hello, Ivy, any changes to report? Any falls?"

"No, nothing. You know what? I've decided that my favorite vegetable is kale. And I like broccoli second."

"Yes, I see that. According to your diary, you're eating several cups of greens a day. And I see you like bananas, blueberries and apples too. You're eating the entire rainbow of foods. Good for you."

"Dr. Grant, our Ivy is a role model for the rest of the family. We're all eating better," said Charlotte.

"And what about stress?" Dr. Grant continued. "Have you been under any particular stress? In glancing at your diary, I noticed you drew a couple of sad faces. What happened on those days?"

"I wish I had more friends. Those were the days I was feeling lonely."

"Do you have friends in your neighborhood?"

"Just one or two. They go to different schools, though."

"Ivy, how would you like my nurse to call your teacher this afternoon? Maybe there's a girl in your grade with epilepsy who you could meet. Your teacher could reach out to the girl's parents to get permission. Would you like that?"

"Sure, Dr. Grant."

"Great, I'll have my nurse contact your teacher."

***

The following afternoon, Mrs. Andrews, Ivy's teacher, pulled Ivy aside. "Ivy, there's a girl in the classroom next to this one. Her name is Gretta. She's a very good student and she's lots of fun. I think you two might really like each other."

"When can I meet her?"

"She's outside the classroom right now. Come on, I'll introduce you."

"Gretta, I'd like you to meet Ivy. She's one of my students."

In nearly one wild jump across the brown linoleum floor, Gretta charged toward Ivy, with her arms wide open, nearly tripping on her one unlaced purple shoe, Gretta gave Ivy the first of what would be many hugs. "Hello, Ivy, I'm Gretta."

GRETTA

Ivy didn't know what to make of Gretta at first. Gretta bounced toward Ivy, up and down like a gas-powered toy car she'd seen on cartoons. Risk of hurting herself appeared not to have ever crossed Gretta's mind.

The rest of the day seemed to happen in a whirl, and before Ivy knew it, she and Gretta were sharing secrets and planning an outing at the park for Saturday. "I'll get my mom to take us to the Dairy Queen after the park," Ivy promised.

"Oh boy, my favorite Dairy Queen dessert are their blizzards." During their very first talk at school, Ivy learned that Gretta liked to read, draw, and paint. Ivy also learned that Gretta lived only four blocks from her.

"Gretta, maybe after we go to the park, you could come to my house. We could draw and color. I just got some really cool stencils, and I have at least a hundred colored pencils."

"Maybe we could spend the whole day together. My mom thinks I'm a good artist," Gretta said, with perky self-assurance.

***

Ivy and Gretta's day at the park was more fun than Ivy had had in a long time. Charlotte drove both to the Dairy Queen after the park. Watching the two of them warmed her heart as she eyed the two new friends sitting on the bench side-by-side, ankles crossed and swinging their calves back and forth while slurping down their tasty treats. While sitting in the car, Charlotte could hear Ivy and Gretta giggling while talking about everything under the sun.

"Gretta, I can't wait for you to meet my dog. His name is Audie and he's my special miniature schnauzer."

"What makes him special?"

"Audie tells me when I'm going to have a seizure before I have one."

"No way! How does he know?"

"He has a super keen sense of smell. He's been able to alert me every time before my seizure starts. We even have a special trainer who comes to our house. She's helping me train Audie to do special tasks."

"How many seizures have you had?"

"Two."

"Only two? I've had four. Medication helps, but I still have seizures. A few months ago, my doctor told me to try changing what I eat. I quit eating gluten. I think it's helped me so far. I haven't had a seizure in three months."

"What's gluten?"

"It's some sort of protein. It's mostly in bread, so I don't eat regular bread any more. Mom buys me food without it."

"C'mon Gretta, let's go to my house. I want you to meet Audie."

***

As soon as Gretta, the stranger, entered Ivy's home, she was nearly pounced on by a 14 lb., fiercely protective Audie.

"Bark, Bark, Bark, Bark, Bark, Bark," Audie yipped, as if to ask, "Who is this bouncy new young human in my house?" Audie had long ago decided to be the household guard dog and acted as if he were as big as a Great Dane.

"Come here, Audie. This is Gretta. Come here, boy. It's okay. Gretta's my friend."

A timid girl would have run, but not Gretta. Fear was not part of Gretta's world or language. She could hardly wait to pet this frisky and loud bark master.

"Come on, Audie, it's okay, you can say hello to my friend," said Ivy. "Gretta, here's a beef nugget for Audie. It's his favorite."

Gretta eagerly opened her hand, permitting Audie to snatch the delightful kibble from her and chomped on it while he sat next to Ivy. "He's the best dog ever. Every now and then I let my friends pet him and give him a treat. His real job, though, is to stay by my side. I can't wait to show you my new rock painting kit, Gretta. Come on Audie, let's go upstairs."

"Wow, your room is huge!" Gretta said, noticing all of Ivy's art work.

"See this? Mom just bought it for me. We could paint any design on these rocks we want. I just finished this one with a sailboat on it." Gretta couldn't help but notice Ivy's artistic skills. Once Gretta began drawing her favorite, a rainbow, Ivy knew she was a better artist than Gretta. *That's her idea of a rainbow?* Ivy thought to herself, *one of these days, I'm going to show Gretta some of my artistic tricks so she can draw as good as me.*

"Gretta, what happens to you when you have a seizure?"

"I go blank for a while, and sometimes my arms and legs shake."

"Do you get scared?" inquired Ivy.

"Not really. My mom always looks out for me. Afterwards, I usually feel ok. Well, except maybe a little tired. What about you?"

"Once I had my second seizure, my doctor diagnosed me with epilepsy and started me on medicine," said Ivy in a resigned tone.

"Same here. I'm on something called Carbamazepine."

"Me too. I have to see my doctor every few months. His nurse draws my blood on every visit. I don't like needles very much."

"My mom thinks I'm courageous. Mom says I don't let epilepsy slow me down. That makes me feel even more courageous. At least I don't fall down and have a super-seizure like Reilly."

"Who's Reilly?"

"Oh, he goes to our school, too. He calls his seizures grand mal. His entire body shakes, and he loses consciousness. He told me he was playing on monkey bars one day by hanging upside down by his heels. Then he swung backward and hit the back of his head on one of the rungs. A week later he had his first seizure."

"I don't know Reilly."

REILLY

"I'll introduce you to him at school on Monday. He's funny. He and I are special friends because of our epilepsy. He jokes a lot and makes me laugh."

"I could ask him about what it feels like to have the kind of seizures he has, and I could tell him about mine."

"I don't think he likes to talk about his epilepsy, Ivy. Reilly has talked about it when we're alone, but only when he's in the mood. He told me he's afraid he'll have another seizure, but his medication really helps him, too."

***

The following Monday morning, Ivy met Reilly during recess. "Ivy, this is Reilly. Reilly, this is Ivy. She's my new friend."

"Hi Ivy, wanna play ball with us?"

Gretta could tell instantly that Ivy wasn't interested. Ivy had no desire to rough-house with the boys, even if it wasn't that rough. "No thanks, Reilly. We're going to sit and talk instead," said Gretta.

As the two girls walked toward the other side of the playground, Gretta told Ivy more about Reilly. "Reilly's always friendly. He invites everybody to play. That's what I like about him the most. He's kind to me."

"Maybe the three of us could do something together. What about studying?"

"Reilly told me once that he gets a lot of C's, so we could invite him to join us during study hall."

"We could find other things to do, too. I know, why don't you both come to my house. I think Reilly might like Gunner. The four of us could play games outside."

"Sure, Ivy. Let's ask him."

***

More than a year after her second seizure, Ivy experienced her third seizure. It happened just before dinnertime. Fortunately, Audie was by Ivy's side. Audie's nose was again hard at work, nudging Ivy's right calf nervously. Ivy took Audie's cue.

"Mom, help!" Soon Charlotte was at Ivy's side. "Ivy, can you hear me? Can you answer me?"

As if in slow motion, Ivy showed only a slight recognition while turning toward her mom. Ivy reached slowly out to her for comfort. Then, in a matter of a minute or two, Ivy was alert and reached out for a hug. Audie stayed with Ivy, and he too had calmed down.

"Ivy, I'm going to call the nurse now."

Ivy was given an appointment to see Dr. Grant the next day. "Hello, Ivy. I understand you had another seizure yesterday?"

"Yes, Dr. Grant."

"Well, I'm glad you came in. I'll examine you, and then we can talk about what to do next. Have you had any falls in the past couple of months?"

"No falls, Dr. Grant."

"I'll need to check the level of your medication again."

The following day, Dr Grant, Ivy and her mom had a Zoom visit. "Ivy, the level of medication in your blood is on the low end, and I think we should increase your dosage. With someone as young as you, we calculate dosage depending on your weight. You've been in a growth spurt, so it makes sense to increase your dosage. Mrs. Cole, as always, call my office if Ivy notices any side effects. She's been on a fairly low dose anyway, so I don't expect she'll experience anything bothersome."

***

"Hi, Olivia! I can't wait to show you what Audie has learned."

"Have you been giving him tons of treats when he obeys you?"

"I sure have. Now he adores me. He doesn't leave my side for a second. He's my little angel watching over me whenever I'm home."

"Let's review what you've already taught him. Then I'll teach you how to train Audie to watch you, a command to get him to turn his attention back to you if he gets distracted, and how to tell him to go down and stay."

On command, Audie, in hot pursuit of his beef kibble, eagerly did whatever Ivy told him. "Come, Audie, good boy," as he gobbled his treat. "Olivia, I had another seizure, and Audie nudged my calf again, so mom gave him a treat afterwards."

"Sorry to hear that, but Audie came to your rescue again? Wow, that's remarkable. It sounds to me that our strategy to use positive reinforcement with Audie has worked. I believe that teaching dogs by rewarding them with something they love is a low-stress fun approach that gives the best results."

"Olivia, Ivy and I followed your advice to the letter," added Charlotte, "We practiced with Audie several times a day for only three or four minutes each time, and we were careful not to give him a total of too much food."

"I'm learning a lot too, Olivia," said Ivy, "Audie's my best friend now."

"That's good news. Let's get to work with Audie, shall we? Is he hungry?"

"He sure is. I cut his breakfast in half. I think he'll do just about anything you ask him to."

"A fun game that I think Audie will learn quickly is a command that both of you can practice several times a day. I want you to say Audie's name, show him the treat, and then say 'Look at me,' while holding the treat up right between your eyes. Audie should stare at his treat for just a second, then reward him with the treat. When he takes it, tell him he's a good boy. When Audie masters staring at the treat, increase the time by having the treat up by your eyes, then very slowly move the treat toward Audie. Because his kibble is getting closer to him, he'll be motivated to continue to stare at the treat. To him, it'll be more exciting because his treat is getting closer. Let's give it a try."

After several trials, Ivy and Audie were hard at work together and learning something new. "Like this, Olivia?"

"Yes, perfect. You rewarded Audie at just the right time. Later, you'll want to hold the treat up by your eyes for two seconds. When he's mastered that, increase the time by an additional second, then another, until Audie holds his stare for twenty or more seconds. It's important that you do this gradually, or you might both get frustrated and lose interest."

"How will this help, Olivia?" Charlotte asked.

"This is an important command to get Audie's attention back to Ivy. For example, she might be outside with Audie when he sees something that distracts him. Ivy then should say, 'Watch me' and redirect him back to her. He's interested in his treat, and he'll learn to ignore the distraction until the temptation goes away."

"He'll be full of treats," Ivy laughed.

"Well, that's a good point, Ivy," said Olivia, "I want you to practice and reward

Audie with a treat each time, and do this for about a month. By then you can begin to wean him off of the treats by rewarding him every other time, and practice it that way for at least a half year."

"What about teaching Audie to stay?" asked both Ivy and her mother.

"To teach Audie to stay, you can add a correction to his training, but only if he doesn't obey."

"What's a correction?"

"A correction is a slight tug on the leash or saying 'No.'"

"How do we know when to correct Audie?"

"My theory is that most of Audie's training should be fun and done through positive rewards. But if you're at the park with Audie, and he sees a squirrel that he'd rather chase, he might give chase and then run the risk of being hit by a car."

"I'd hate for that to happen," exclaimed Ivy.

"That's why practicing corrections are valuable. Many trainers believe that coupling positive and negative together elicits a more desirable and consistent response than positive rewards alone. Deciding what type of response will work can be tricky. Be patient, but be consistent. The two best approaches are a quick tug on the leash, or simply saying 'No' to Audie should work best. That doesn't mean you should yell or punish him or jerk his leash so hard that it hurts him."

"Thanks for your help, Olivia. Ivy and I will start training Audie today," said Charlotte.

"Now I've learned what to say to him and why," said Ivy.

***

Ivy's medications controlled her seizures through the rest of grade school and middle school. By the time she was thirteen, Ivy had hoped that her epilepsy was gone from her life forever.

It'd been eighteen months since her last seizure and Ivy, Gretta, and Reilly had become the fearsome threesome. They ate lunch together and whispered constantly during study hall. "Shhh, you three," said Mr. Thompson, the study hall monitor. This stopped them for mere minutes before they were at it again.

***

A few months later while at home, Ivy exhibited signs of another seizure. Audie bolted upright once again, and fixing a nervous stare at Ivy, he inched closer to her and nudged and pawed at her leg. He then put his front legs on her lap so he could stare directly into Ivy's face. Audie began to bark. Ivy's family dropped everything they were doing and ran into the living room. Ivy was having her fourth seizure. This time, Ivy's seizure did not end quickly and seemed to progress with greater intensity. The seizure seemed to have its grips on Ivy's whole body with more shakiness than on previous occasions. Thankfully, the nightmare came to a swift end.

"Ivy, do you know where you are?"

"Yes, Mom. I'm home, with you and Dad, Gunner and Audie."

"Did you realize what was happening?"

"I can't remember anything."

"I think you should see Dr. Grant as soon as possible. Your seizure seemed worse this time."

***

At the doctor's office the following day, Ivy reported feeling the same sensation of jiggles, followed by an upset stomach and an inability to respond to her name being called. "Ivy, has anything changed in your life?" inquired nurse Jenna.

"I've been doing really well, Jenna."

"You're at about at the age when a lot of girls begin having their periods. You're going through hormonal changes, and those changes sometimes trigger seizures."

"Really? I didn't know that. I started getting my period a couple of months ago."

"I'll let Dr. Grant know. He'll discuss it with you. He might need to adjust your medication."

"Ivy, good to see you," Dr. Grant said as he entered the exam room, closing the door behind him. "How are you feeling today?" conveying his usual reassuring smile.

"I had another seizure. Mom said she thought this one was worse. I felt tired last night after my seizure so I went to bed early. Audie stayed by my side the rest of the night. I woke up this morning feeling fine, like nothing had happened."

"I've double-checked your blood draw from last week, and it's about in the middle of the range. I think it's also time to do another EEG on you. Your hormones change at the time of your monthly cycle, and that change could've triggered your seizure. There are medications that you could take during your period. But before we do that, I want you to keep track of how you feel before and after each period in your diary for a few months."

"What if Ivy has another seizure?" Charlotte said, "She had us pretty worried last night."

"Then call me immediately or take her to the emergency room. I can also send you home with a prescription that can help her recover, and she might not need an emergency room visit."

"A drug to help?"

"Yes, it's a benzodiazepine. It'll calm the neurons in her brain. Ivy, overall, you've been managing well. I'm really proud of you for keeping such a good diary. Many of my patients don't get enough rest. You seem to be averaging nine hours a night of sleep, and I'm sure this has helped. You're growing and your body is changing, so I might need to adjust or change your medication as you change."

"Thanks, Dr. Grant."

"Anything in particular that you're looking for with the EEG, Doctor?" pressed Charlotte.

"I want to check if there's been a change in the type of seizure Ivy had last night."

Within the hour, Dr. Grant had reviewed Ivy's EEG. "Ivy, there's been a change with this last seizure. It looks like what you experienced is something I call a secondarily generalized seizure."

"What does that mean?"

"I think your seizure started in one part of your brain and then spread to the other part of your brain. I'd like to try a different medicine with you. The name of the drug is Keppra. I think Keppra is better suited to your situation. Similar to your current med, this one has the potential for side effects, too."

"Like what, Doctor?

"I want you to pay attention to whether or not you feel more anxious or angry. Also, if you feel dizzy or have diarrhea, have headaches or joint pain, please let me know. There are actually several side effects; I'll send you home with a complete fact sheet to read through."

"Is it hard to switch medications?"

"It should be pretty easy. You'll start taking the new medication while you're still on your current medication. Will you give it a try?"

"Sure, Doctor, I'll do whatever you think is best."

"Great, I'd like to start you on 500 mg twice a day. It's important to use your diary to jot down any changes in how you feel both physically and emotionally, okay?"

"I'll remind her, Doctor," said Charlotte. "Is there anything else I can do to help?"

"Yes, you can watch Ivy and tell me if you notice any changes in her behavior.

You can take Keppra with or without food, but whichever you do, I recommend you take it the same way and the same time each day."

"Dr. Grant, I have a few more questions about how we can help Ivy when she has her period. Is she really at risk of having another seizure at the same time every month? If that's true, is there anything we can do to help?"

"That's partly why I'm switching her to Keppra. If necessary, we can increase her dose a few days before her menstrual cycle. With Keppra, I'll need to continue checking her blood level. There's an additional medication that some of my patients take just at the time of their period. But this isn't a sure-fire solution and works best in women who have regular cycles. I don't want to make too many changes at once. That's where her diary will be helpful."

"Thank you, Dr. Grant. We'll take the new prescriptions and read up on both of them."

***

"I had another seizure last week." Gretta whispered to Ivy at school the following Monday."

"Why didn't you tell me earlier?"

"I didn't want to upset you. I've had more seizures than you. In fact, my doctor put me on a second medication."

"Gretta, you're taking two now?"

"Yep. My doctor hopes to find the right medication to completely control my seizures. Wouldn't that be great? I'd love to do whatever I want without worrying about having a seizure. I prefer to think about the good things I have going for me. I want to spend time with you, paint, and go to the movies like everyone else. I plan to live a normal life, including studying hard so I can go to college."

"Gretta, you're my hero. I don't know what I'd do if I didn't have you to talk to. You make all of my days better."

"I'll always be your friend. Hey, I have an idea. Why don't you and I be college roomies?" said Gretta. "Best friends forever," they both chimed.

"Gretta, I had another seizure last week, too. And this one was worse. Dr. Grant is changing me over to a new medication. He thinks this one will help me the most. It's called Keppra.

"Do you think Dr. Grant is changing your medication because you're getting older?"

"Well, that too, but he also said that my last seizure was something he called generalized. That means it spread through my whole brain."

***

Ivy, Gretta and Reilly were excited about starting tenth grade. On the first day at their new school, they stayed in close contact with each other in order to courageously face the sea of strangers in the large high school. Their first day at school navigating locker combinations, stares from girls who'd already defined their own clique, finding each new class, and the maze of new teachers had created an emotional tidal wave for all three of them.

"I hope the three of us are in a lot of classes together," said Ivy.

"Me too," said Gretta and Reilly in unison.

"Let's stick by each other. I'm a little scared," said Ivy, "What if one of us has a seizure?"

"We'll be labeled as the kids who have fits," said Reilly.

"I'd just die if that happened," said Ivy.

"Who cares," defended Gretta, "We'll stare right back at them and tell them we have epilepsy. I'm not going to be self-conscious about it, and I promise, I'll take care of you. We should all talk to the nurse, too."

"What if some of the kids are mean?" said Ivy.

"I'll be by your side," said Gretta.

"I want to fit in," said Reilly. "I plan to check out what clubs I can join. I feel fine, and I'm not going to worry about epilepsy."

"What clubs, Reilly?" said Ivy. "Maybe I can join too."

"I was thinking about tennis. I started practicing over the summer, and it was fun."

"I just want to make friends," said Gretta, "I'm curious about track. Ivy, you could join too."

"Ok, Gretta," said Ivy, "But It'll take me a while to get used to my new classes. Maybe later. I don't want to jump into anything and then feel stressed out about it. Besides, I've got Audie at home to help me get my physical exercise."

"Ivy, you haven't had any seizures in a long time. Don't worry too much. If you find a club you like, I think you should look into it," encouraged Gretta.

Later that day, the three rendezvoused for lunch. They talked about their new homeroom teachers, and all agreed that they found homeroom helpful. They'd not known what books to get, and their homeroom teacher helped direct them through the list.

Once home, Ivy had a lot to tell her mom about her first day. "Mom, Gretta and Reilly and I stuck together. We promised we'd take care of each other. As soon as one of us begins to feel lonely or left out, the other two will come to the rescue. We're in the same lunch period. We talked about what would happen if one of us has a seizure. It helped to talk about it, and we calmed each other down. After lunch, the rest of my day went well."

Charlotte and Donovan had been concerned about Ivy starting a new school and especially about being a teenager with epilepsy. Charlotte spent sleepless nights concerned about Ivy and had talked with Donovan and Dr. Grant about her worries.

"Char," said Donovan, "We've done a great job with Ivy, but there'll still be challenges and surprises. Ivy's a good kid, but she'll make mistakes. She'll learn."

"I'm concerned about her, Donovan. What if someone makes fun of her? I worry that she'll feel lonely and begin to isolate."

"Ivy has Gretta to talk with. And Reilly too. Ivy has to navigate her way into adulthood, and she can't do it if you're hovering over her like a helicopter mom, acting like she can't take care of herself."

"If only she didn't have epilepsy," Char sighed. "I watched my sister struggle all her life with this. I don't want Ivy to go through the same thing."

"Ivy does have epilepsy. It's not our epilepsy; it's Ivy's disease and as she grows up, she'll learn how to manage it. I'd be more worried if her seizures were uncontrolled, but her medications are working. Look how well she's done with eating healthy and keeping her diary. Dr. Grant has said that Ivy is one of the most compliant patients he's ever had. Have a little faith in her."

"But it's the peer pressure. That can be brutal. I want to keep Ivy safe."

"Look, Char, we'll just have to pay attention and listen to her when she comes to us for help. She's a smart girl, and if she does something wrong or feels embarrassed about something, we'll just have to trust that she'll come to us."

"Being a teen is hard enough, but what about drinking, drug use, getting in with the wrong crowd?" Char sighed.

"So far Ivy isn't in the wrong crowd. If you're that worried about her, maybe we should talk to her about getting involved in clubs at school. I think theater would be fun. She might really like that."

"Wow, what a good idea. I'll ask Ivy about it."

"Dr. Grant has already cautioned Ivy about activities that she should avoid."

"Yeah, and thankfully she's not interested in them anyway. She couldn't care less about the high-risk stuff like hang-gliding, skydiving, or rock-climbing."

"We already know she gets enough exercise."

"She mentioned taking swim lessons the other day. I'd like to talk to Dr. Grant about this first."

"Let's let Ivy take charge of her own life. Tell Ivy to talk to Dr. Grant herself. We don't have to step in and do everything for her."

***

"Gretta, you interested in the dance at school next Friday night?" inquired Ivy.

"Maybe just for something to do. Why? Do you want to go?"

"I've never been to a dance. The other kids in my homeroom are going."

"Then let's go. If we don't like it, we can always call our parents for a ride home. Let's ask Reilly to go too."

"What should we wear?"

"I don't have a thing. Nothing cool, anyway. Maybe our moms could drop us off at the mall tomorrow."

Ivy, Reilly and Gretta realized quickly that none of them really knew how to dance. Sure, they all liked Taylor Swift, Billie Eilish and Dua Lipa, but how to dance to their music? None of them really had a clue.

"Reilly, Gretta and I are going to get you on the dance floor if no one asks us to dance. You'll be our go-to guy, okay?"

"No problem. I was thinking the same thing. I don't want to ask a girl to dance and have her make a face at me."

***

Once at the school auditorium, Gretta and Ivy ducked into the bathroom to check make-up and gather their nerves. But they weren't prepared for the surprise that was going on in the back of the bathroom.

"Hey you guys, come on back here."

"What's going on?" asked Gretta.

"Janet brought some of her parent's liquor. We've got wine, peppermint schnapps, or if you're ready for the hard stuff, we've got some brandy. Have a drink."

As Gretta, reached her hand out to give the schnapps a try, Ivy grabbed her arm. "No thanks, Janet. Maybe some other time."

"Suit yourself."

Once out of earshot, Ivy stared at Gretta critically, "What the hell were you thinking?"

"Chill, Ivy, I was just trying to get along with friends. One taste isn't going to kill us."

"Our doctors said no drinking, remember?"

"Yeah, but we don't really know that for sure. May we could have one drink without it throwing us into a seizure."

"Oh really? And you want to take that risk? You want to go home by way of the ambulance? Really, Gretta, have you lost your flippin' mind? We came here to hang with our friends and do some dancing, not start drinking. We don't even know what's really in the bottle, do we?"

"Okay, okay, Ivy. I hear you. Let's just dance. Forget I even brought it up."

***

"How was the dance, Ivy? Did you and Gretta have fun? Do you think you'll go to the next one?" asked Charlotte.

"We had a great time, mom. We danced a lot but mostly with Reilly. We laughed a lot and had fun with some of the kids in our classes. Some of them were in theater, and they think I should audition for a part in the next play, so I might give it a try."

"Your dad and I were thinking the same thing. Acting could be really fun."

"Something else happened when we first got to the dance. A few girls were in the bathroom drinking some booze, and they were pushing Gretta and me to drink with them."

"What happened? What did you tell them?"

"Gretta wanted to give it a try. She said one little drink wouldn't hurt. I told her I thought she was wrong, and I dragged her out of the bathroom. She never brought it up again the rest of the night. In fact, the girls who were drinking were caught and thrown out of school. Another girl got sick and puked her guts out. She made a fool of herself. I'm glad I wasn't anywhere near her, or I would've gotten into trouble right along with her. I heard they might get suspended."

"You did the right thing, Ivy. Epilepsy and drinking simply do not mix. You don't need to test what Dr. Grant has already told you."

"I was thinking, mom, that I'd like to meet and talk with other people who are dealing with epilepsy. Gretta and Reilly are great, but I'd like to meet and talk with more people who have epilepsy."

"I think I might have the perfect solution. Why don't you call Dr. Grant's office and ask them whether or not they have a group for people with epilepsy."

***

The next day, Ivy emailed Dr. Grants office inquiring about a support group. Jenna quickly responded, informing her of a new group at the clinic's office the following evening at 7 pm. Ivy registered immediately, then called Gretta.

"Gretta, there's a support group for people with epilepsy tomorrow night at my doctor's office. Why don't you join me?"

"What'll I have to do? Why do you want to go?"

"I don't know a whole lot yet. I'll figure that out after the first meeting. My doctor's nurse said it's a place for people with epilepsy to talk about their journey and how they cope."

"How much does it cost?"

"The group is free. All you have to do is register. Come on, Gretta, just try it once."

"Ok, it might be fun. Something new to do."

"It starts at 7 pm. Mom and I will pick you up and drive you back home."

***

Ivy and Gretta arrived early for the meeting. Both had tried to convince Reilly to join them, but he said support groups were too touchy-feely for him and decided it wasn't his thing.

"Welcome, everyone. We have two newcomers tonight, Ivy and Gretta."

After a quick round of friendly hellos, the facilitator, Mark, a mental health intern, outlined what the group was about. "This is a safe place to share and to talk. This is a no-judgement zone. We're here to share stories and to remind yourselves that epilepsy does not define you. We're not here to give advice. We're here to listen empathetically. Only share something about yourself that you feel comfortable sharing. If you want to just sit and listen, that is perfectly fine, too."

The group was a welcome relief for Ivy. "Gretta, I really liked meeting all of the new people tonight. I especially liked meeting a couple of the older adults. They were really kind and patient. I learned a lot."

"Me, too. Listening to the others helped me to stop thinking about my own problems. Some of the group members had some pretty horrific stories yet they stay tough. It was really hard to listen to the woman talk about her surgery."

"Yeah, but at the same time, I'm glad I heard it. I gave her a hug after the group. Gretta, you and I have a lot to be grateful for. Even if our medications don't work a hundred percent, I doubt we'll ever need surgery."

"I sure hope not. The main thing that going to this group did for me tonight was to remind me that I'm not alone in this. That, and feeling tons of gratitude."

"Does that mean we're going to continue to attend?"

"Yeah, Ivy, let's keep going. I actually enjoyed it."

***

As Ivy, Gretta, and Reilly settled in to high school life, they were ready for new challenges, new activities, and had made new friends. Reilly had decided to join the baseball team and seemed happier than ever. To their delight, all three friends shared at least two classes together: health and speech.

"Class, can I have your attention, please? Raise your hands if you've ever heard of something called meditation," said Mrs. Andrews.

Not a single hand went up. Taking notice, their teacher said, "I'd like to begin teaching meditation in class."

"What is it, Mrs. Andrews?" chimed in several of the boys.

"Mostly, it's learning to relax using techniques of visualization and deep-breathing. The other teachers and I have been talking about fitting it into our class schedule a few times every week."

"Sure, Mrs. Andrews, as long as there's no homework."

"No, Jimmy," Mrs. Andrews smiled, "We'll always do it together as a class. I promise you it's easy to learn. And you might even find out that it can help you with sports. For those of you in the class that have particular medical issues, come and talk to me at the end of class. I may need you to get permission from your doctors first."

***

"Mom, what's meditation? My health teacher wants us to learn and practice it during class. She says she meditates every day."

"Has she started teaching it yet?"

"No. Today she just asked us if we were interested. Nearly all of us agreed.

She also said I needed to show her a note from Dr. Grant stating I can do it."

"Well, most people do it for health reasons. Like lowering their blood pressure and sleeping better. But there're all kinds of reasons people like to meditate."

"Do you meditate, mom?"

"I meditate every day if I have the time. I try to do it right after lunch. I have my own tape that I listen to. I sit in my chair in the den."

"How long does it take?"

"Well, Ivy, the CD that I listen to talks about how remarkable our bodies are. It only lasts about ten minutes. I take a deep breath to the count of four, then I exhale to the count of five. I repeat this several times. While breathing, I visualize my favorite peaceful place, like sitting on the beach by the ocean."

"My teacher says she loves to meditate, too."

"It's kind of like daydreaming. You take slow, deep breaths. As you focus on something specific, you stop thinking about all of the other things going on around you that might worry you. It'll help you to stay relaxed, and maybe in some way it will help with your epilepsy. I'm sure it's not a cure, but it is one way to decrease stress. I'm glad she's cautious about getting you started in class. We definitely need to talk to Dr. Grant first."

"Do you think I'll like it? What if my classmates complain about it?"

"Honey, meditation is something you can do by yourself and anywhere you want. It takes practice; I don't expect it to be super great the first time you try it. You and I could meditate together on the weekends if you like."

"Gretta's a ball of energy all day long. Maybe relaxing in the middle of the day will help her, too."

"Gretta and you might both learn to love it. But Gretta and her mom will also need to talk to Gretta's doctor first."

***

"Dr. Grant, I'd like to talk with you about meditation. My mom does it, and now my teacher wants us to practice it in class. I need a permission slip from you," said Ivy.

"Ivy, meditation can be a great activity to improve overall health and decrease stress," replied Dr. Grant.

"Why do I need to talk with you and get permission?"

"Because there's some concern that meditation could also trigger a seizure. Managing stress is very important, but meditation also changes the activity in your brain. There's not a lot of studies done yet about the effects of meditation on children and teens."

"Mom meditates, and she says it's rewarding."

"The simple act of deep breathing brings about complex changes in the brain," said Dr. Grant. "In your case, because your seizures have been infrequent, I see no problem in giving it a try. I'll write you a permission slip, but I'm going to put a time limit on it. Then let's talk again in a couple of months to review your experience with it. Meanwhile, make notes in your diary about any effects meditation has had on your daily activities and feelings. I'd also like you to limit your meditation to ten minutes a day."

"Just ten minutes?" a surprised Ivy said.

"Yes, Ivy, ten minutes is enough time for you to feel the benefits of meditation. When we meet again, we can talk about lengthening the time if you like it and want to continue."

Benefits of Meditation

Relaxation through deep breathing

- Helps reduce stress
- Can be done alone or in a group
- Easy to teach to friends
- Doesn't cost anything & can be done anywhere
- Improves sleep
- Improves blood pressure
- Increases self-awareness
- Focuses on the present
- Reduces negative emotions
- Increases imagination and creativity
- Increases patience and tolerance

Caution: Patients with epilepsy should always consult their physician before beginning activities such as meditation, yoga, or mindfulness training. Every person with epilepsy experiences seizures in their own unique way, and guidance from a physician is strongly recommended by healthcare professionals.

***

"Ivy, come here, I've got something to show you," Gretta said with a mischievous glimmer in her eye. Gretta grabbed Ivy's arm and eagerly shepherded Ivy to a hidden place around the corner by their school.

"What is it, Gretta?"

"A girl in my neighborhood gave me a joint last night. She said pot helps stop seizures. Let's light it up."

"I've never smoked before, and I've never thought about it. What if we get sick? What if we get caught?"

While pulling out the white, hand-rolled, crumpled three-inch long smokable object, Gretta, said, "We could just try a little. Just to see how it feels."

"I don't know, Gretta. What if we really do get sick or forget where we are? What if we both have a seizure?"

"I hadn't thought of that," sighed Gretta.

"It sounds like a stupid mistake. I've heard that pot has other chemicals in it, too. What if there's something bad in it?"

"You know, Ivy, sometimes you can be a little dull. Don't you have any guts at all? If anything happens, we can always help each other."

"It seems to me that the easiest way to get answers is to talk with my doctor during my next visit."

"God no, don't do that! You know he'll tell you to stick with your medication. He might even put you on more. Then he'll tell your mom. Then you'll tell on me!"

"Gretta, I've never smoked anything before. I don't like smoke. Dr. Grant said I shouldn't smoke cigarettes, and pot is probably even worse. I'd be crazy to put that junk into my lungs."

"Ok, we don't have to try it yet, but just remember that I have it. If you change your mind, we can try it. It'll be our secret. I had another seizure last night, and I'm ready to try anything."

"Did you tell your mom? What did she do?"

"I was in my bedroom. I didn't even tell her."

"Gretta, you have to tell your mom everything. She can't help you otherwise."

"I know the drill, Ivy. Sometimes I think I'm never going to get epilepsy out of my life."

"I had a small seizure recently, too. I didn't want to talk about it either, but I changed my mind and told my mom. I called my doctor the next day. He didn't make any changes and he was reassuring. Dr. Grant has told me a bunch of times that many teens are able to get off their meds permanently, Gretta. Promise me you won't try this joint by yourself."

"Okay, Okay. I promise. I'll see you tomorrow."

After saying goodbye, Ivy felt a tinge of sadness about Gretta. And about epilepsy, for that matter. And for herself. *How bad will my seizure disorder get? Will I be able to say goodbye to epilepsy someday? Will I ever be able to drink alcohol or smoke pot? Probably not.* Ivy was filled with thoughts about the lifelong effects of epilepsy and how it had enveloped her life so far. Then again, if she didn't have epilepsy, she would not have Gretta as her best friend, and she would not have met all of the kind and generous people in the support group.

By the time Ivy arrived home, she was craving her usual attention from Audie. Gunner bounced toward Ivy, too, as if he'd been waiting forever to see her."

"Ivy, Ivy, let's go outside and play catch."

"I don't feel like it, Gunner. I need to spend time with Audie. I've got lots of homework, too." Audie was already on his back, legs flailing in the air, mouth wide open, as if to show Ivy his big smile while getting his biggest belly rub of the day.

"What's wrong, Ivy?" Gunner groaned.

"Do you know what a joint is, Gunner? Gretta tried to get me to smoke one with her after school today. I didn't want to, and I told her so. I'm scared she'll keep pushing me. Gretta told me she thought I was dull. I don't want to be dull."

"Don't listen to her, Ivy. What about your seizures?"

"Gretta thinks marijuana might stop them from happening."

"Is that true?"

"I told her, 'No", but I'm scared she'll stop being my friend if I don't give in."

"What are you going to do?"

"I haven't decided yet. I'm going to my room to start my homework."

***

"Mom, Mom. Ivy told me that Gretta wanted her to smoke pot with her on the way home from school today," said Gunner.

Nearly dropping the hotdish while removing it from the oven, Charlotte flashed a startled glance at Gunner. "What did you say?"

"That's what she told me, Mom."

"What happened?"

"Ivy said no, but she might change her mind and try it anyway."

"Where's Ivy now?"

"She's in her room studying."

***

"Ivy, can I come in?" Charlotte said, while opening the door, as if saying 'No' was not an option.

"Sure, mom, what's wrong?"

"Gunner just told me Gretta asked you to smoke pot with her."

"He shouldn't have told you! Besides, I said no. What's the big deal?"

"The big deal is that we need to talk about this. The big deal is that you have epilepsy. The big deal is that just doing a little could harm you."

"Mom, I said no. I'm too scared to try it."

"There are so many unknown and dangerous chemicals in street drugs that you never know what's in them. Dealers don't care what they're selling. If Fentanyl is in it, it'll kill you. You have no idea where Gretta got this stuff."

"She got it from a neighbor."

"That guarantees nothing, Ivy. Maybe Gretta isn't such a great friend after all."

"Mom, don't say that. She's my best friend. We plan to go to college together."

"Let's talk to Dr. Grant next week about this. He's probably discussed this hundreds of times with his patients."

"I wish you'd just trust me. I wasn't going to do anything to hurt myself."

"I do, Ivy, but I'm still your mother, and I'm going to worry about you. Dinner will be ready in a half hour, and we're going to tell Dr. Grant," Charlotte said, patting Ivy on her leg, and giving Audie an extra scratch to his ears.

Biting her lower lip and furrowing her brows together, Ivy decided she was going to give Gunner a piece of her mind. Banging on Gunner's bedroom door, "Gunner," as she flung the door open, "Thanks for ratting me out. What'd you do that for?"

"I don't want you to get hurt."

"I can take care of myself. Now Mom's on my case. I have to talk to Dr. Grant about this now. Thanks a lot."

"I wanna come with when you see Dr. Grant. I wanna know what he says. Ivy, I don't want you to have another seizure," said Gunner, on the verge of tears and lower lip quivering.

***

With the whole family in tow, Mom, Dad, Gunner and Ivy sat patiently in Dr. Grant's office for one of her routine visits. Ivy had been to his office a few days earlier for her blood draw and was eager to hear the results.

"Hello, Ivy. Good to see you. I see you've brought your whole family. Is everything all right?"

"Everything's fine, Doctor. I haven't had any seizures. I've been keeping up with my diary. I've been eating vegetables every day, and I go to bed every night by 8:30. Oh, and I'm getting all A's."

"Glad to hear that. Your blood work looks great. Your Keppra level is just where we want it. Unless you disagree, I think we should keep you on the same dosage. Any other questions?"

"Dr. Grant, we want to talk with you about marijuana. Ivy's best friend asked Ivy to smoke pot with her last week. Thankfully, Ivy refused. I'm worried that it's only a matter of time before she tries it." Charlotte said, with a noticeable quiver in her voice. "We wanted to talk about this with you today. That's why the whole family is here."

As curious as Ivy was, she felt ratted out once again and sat stiffly, both arms crossed and resting on her chest, shooting a glance of embarrassment at her mother.

"Ivy, I talk about this with my patients every day. I'm not surprised in the least that a friend would show you a joint. Did a close friend tell you it would help your seizures?"

Straightening up in her chair and unclasping her hands, Ivy's interest was piqued. "That's exactly what my friend told me. How did you know?"

"Ivy, there's a lot of misconceptions about marijuana and epilepsy. THC in street marijuana is the chemical compound that makes you high and I would never recommend to my patients that they use this, no matter how old they are. Did your friend pressure you?"

"Yes, she did. It was Gretta. She comes with me to the support group here sometimes. When I said 'No', she told me I was dull."

"Ivy, you showed a lot of strength by saying no. Gretta might not have told you that she saw your courage, but she'll never forget it."

"A lot of kids in school are smoking pot. I don't know what excuse I can give without them making fun of me."

"Ivy, the other doctors and I are hearing this from our patients. We've gotten concerned enough that we've decided to call our patients together to discuss marijuana. It'll be on Saturday the 15th, next month. I'd like you all to come."

"We'll be there," said Donovan and Charlotte, "You can count on it."

"Good, I'll get you registered. In the meantime, I've developed a chart about marijuana and related drugs. I'll give you a copy now if you like. And please tell Gretta that she and her family are welcome to attend, too.

Quick-reference Chart: Cannabis-related terms, Marijuana, and Cannabinoids.					
Name	What Is It? Source?	Varieties	Recreational Information	Medical Or Scientific Info	Legal Restrictions
Cannabis	Generic term for products from the plant.	Source of fiber, food, oil and medicine	High potential for abuse to induce euphoria & relaxation.	Classified as Schedule I; not accepted for medical use	Not federally legal; Laws vary by state. https://www.ncsl.org/research/health/state-medical-marijuana-laws.aspx
Marijuana (MJ)	It is the whole plant, i.e., flowers, leaves, stems, seeds.	Dried mixture of leaves and flowers	RM – term for recreational marijuana	Lack of placebo-controlled studies	Drug Enforcement Agency (DEA) recently affirmed it as a class I substance. See note below.
THC Tetrahydro-cannabinol	Active ingredient that induces feeling of euphoria.	Is available in several forms, including oils, edibles and capsules.	Smoking MJ contains similar compounds as tobacco, so there are concerns about lung health.	Considered a Gateway drug for abuse of and addiction to other drugs.	Under current federal law there is no legal means to obtain marijuana for medical use. Violators of federal law risk prosecution, imprisonment, fines, and forfeiture of property.
Hemp	Historically grown for fiber found in stalks and seeds	Minimal amount of THC	Hemp cannot contain more than 0.3 % THC. Anything with more THC is classified as MJ, a schedule 1 drug.	Used for constipation and high cholesterol. There is no good scientific evidence to support use.	Flowering portions extracted from hemp plants are considered marijuana and are classified as a schedule I substance. Don't confuse hemp with Canadian hemp, hemp agrimony, cannabis, or cannabidiol (CBD).
Hemp Oil	An oil extracted from cannabis seeds by cold pressing.	Contains only trace amounts of cannabinoids and terpenes.	Used in paints, varnishes, soap and a variety of food products.	High in unsaturated fatty acids.	In 2018, hemp was officially legalized on the federal level.
Cannabinoid (CBD)	Term used to refer to molecules found in the cannabis plant.	Over 100 naturally occurring chemicals found in the plant.	Not believed to be psycho-active.	Classified as phytocan-nabinoids, endocan-nabinoids or synthetic cannabinoid.	CBD can have no more than 0.3 percent THC to be legal at the federal level.
CBD	One of the major cannabin-oids derived from cannabis.	Gummies, sold at specialty shops,	Has been used to improve sleep. Doesn't help to fall asleep, and reports that results don't last.	The Cannabidiol Epidiolex was approved in 2018 for treating seizures. *	Controlled CBD preparation that meets standards of purity, consistency, stability, safety, and efficacy. It can be plant-derived or synthetic.

Quick-reference Chart: Cannabis-related terms, Marijuana, and Cannabinoids.					
Name	What Is It? Source?	Varieties	Recreational Information	Medical Or Scientific Info	Legal Restrictions
CBD Oil	Extracted from the flowering portions of the hemp plant and dissolved in another oil.	Contains no THC, has no psycho-active properties.	Although CBD is generally safe, it can cause adverse effects such as diarrhea and fatigue.	CBD oil interacts with certain medications, causing harmful side effects.	Hemp and CBD oil are federally legal in all 50 states. Anyone in the US can legally buy CBD oil on health store shelves, some pet stores, and the internet.
Cannabis Oil	Concentra-ted cannabis extracts	Often contains very high levels of THC.	Risk of addiction is higher when use starts as a teen, because the brain is not finished developing until age 25.	Heavy cannabis use among young users can lead to learning impairments.	It can also lead to changes in personality, judgment, and reasoning skills.
Terpenes / Terpenoids	Primary aromatic principles found in cannabis.	Provides the scent and flavor.	Aromatic compound found in many plants, such as lavender.	None	Legal because they contain no THC. Generally recognized as safe by the FDA for use in foods.
Food And Drug Administration (FDA)	Federal agency of the Health and Human Services Division	Takes several years to approve a drug for market.	Interest in the utility of cannabis to treat a variety of conditions, as well as potential adverse health effects.	FDA has not approved a marketing application for cannabis for the treatment of any condition.	The FDA does not control dietary or over-the-counter supplements. The FDA is the center for drug evaluation and research. www.fda.gov.

The FDA is aware that unapproved cannabis and/or unapproved cannabis-derived products are being used to treat a number of medical conditions including: AIDS wasting, epilepsy, neuropathic pain, spasticity associated with multiple sclerosis, and cancer and chemotherapy-induced nausea. However, the use of unapproved cannabis and cannabis-derived products can have unpredictable and unintended consequences, including serious safety risks. There has been no FDA review of data from rigorous clinical trials to support that these unapproved products are safe for the various therapeutic uses for which they are being used.

*The FDA has approved Epidiolex, which contains a purified from of the drug substance cannabidiol (CBD) for the treatment of seizures associated with Lennox-Gastaut syndrome or Dravet syndrome in patients 2 years of age and older.

***

The Cole family, and Gretta and her mother were eager to attend Dr. Grant's lecture.

"Ivy, I learned a lot today. Dr. Grant and his team were nice to us. They didn't give a scary lecture about street drugs. They just gave us the facts."

"Not only that, Gretta, they treated us like adults. If I want to use medical marijuana, I'm going to talk with Dr. Grant first. I think everyone in my family learned a lot, too."

"I guess I won't go running off on my own to treat my seizures. The idea to smoke that joint was lame," said Gretta. "I didn't tell you earlier, but I asked Reilly to smoke that joint with me, too."

"I take it he said no?"

"Reilly said he would never touch pot. He said he was disappointed in me. Then he chewed me out. He said the same thing as you; that pot is laced with too many dangerous chemicals."

"Good for him."

"It's too bad he missed this lecture today. I'm going to give him a copy of the handouts. I know he'll read them."

"I know you get down after you have a seizure, Gretta. So yesterday, I came up with a list of things that I think are really, really important that might help both of us avoid having another seizure. Here, I wrote out the list on a piece of paper for you," Ivy said, while handing it to Gretta.

"This first one is a good idea. I need to keep my medication in plain sight so I don't forget to take my meds. At least one of my seizures was because I missed taking my medication," Gretta said.

"Plus, Gretta, make sure you refill your prescription before you run out. If you or I run out of our meds on a holiday, or the doctor's office or pharmacy is closed, you and I would be in real trouble."

"Here's another thing on the list that I never thought about. Avoid catching colds as much as possible. Getting our annual flu shots is really important, too."

"Right, Gretta. Neither of us need a challenge to our general health. We especially need to avoid getting fevers."

"Ivy, you're always good about eating right. I don't know anyone who eats as many fruits and vegetables as you. Mom's been pushing me to eat bigger salads and she wants me to steam green vegetables for dinner. I think I'll start listening to her."

"Last but not least, Gretta, stress is always going to be in our lives, and we can help each other with this. Promise me, Gretta, that if something is really stressing you out, that you'll talk to me about it."

"I promise," said Gretta, "My doctor gave me the green light to practice meditation, so I'm going to try to do it at least a few times a week, too."

Fact: The number one reported cause of increased seizures is missed medications.

***

"Welcome to speech class, I'll be your teacher and my name is Lucille Roberts. Within the month, you'll all get practice at speaking in front of a group about any topic of your choosing. My only requirement for your talk is that it must be informative. In other words, educate your classmates about a topic they may know very little about."

Nearly everyone in class let out a collective sigh. Except Ivy. Ivy felt nearly blessed. *How easy. This is my chance to tell my friends about my life with epilepsy.* "Ms. Roberts," Ivy's hand raised quickly, eager to get started. "I know exactly what I'm going to talk about."

"I'll bet you do, Ivy. Do you have a question?"

"Can I bring my dog?"

"In your case, Ivy, I'd be thrilled to have your dog as a guest."

"Can I go first?"

"Of course."

One month later, Ivy was ready to give her emotional and most informative speech. As Audie was making a special guest appearance, Ivy would soon learn that she was going to be the most popular girl in her class on this day. Audie needed care and leadership during Ivy's speech, so Ivy's mom brought Audie and was just as excited as Ivy about her talk. Everyone knew ahead of time they were going to learn about epilepsy, and Ivy had been rehearsing her first speech for two weeks.

Ivy stood excitedly in front of thirty classmates. Ivy had set up an easel at the front of the classroom. Her mother and Audie sat in front of the classroom in a chair to Ivy's right. Ivy's classmates were attentive and sat quietly as Ivy stood to begin.

"Uh-hem, I was diagnosed with epilepsy at the age of ten, so I consider myself an expert on the topic. I'd like to tell you what it feels like to have a seizure. I'd like to tell you about my dog, Audie. He has always alerted me before the start of my seizures. I also want to tell you about my healthcare team. All of them have taught me not to be scared and not to let epilepsy control my life. And most of all, I want to talk about how epilepsy has made me a stronger person."

Time flew by. In fact, Ivy's talk took longer than expected, but her teacher decided to let her talk as long as she needed. When finished, her classmates applauded and cheered. Audie wagged his tail and barked. Charlotte brought treats for Ivy's classmates. She also brought treats for Audie, and Ivy showed her fellow students how she had trained Audie to stay by her side and stay focused on her whenever she gave Audie a command.

After speech class, Charlotte drove Ivy, Audie, and Gretta home. "Ivy, that was the best speech in the whole world. Thanks for mentioning me as your best friend," Gretta said.

"I was pretty nervous, but this was my best day ever at school. Gretta, I thought you told the class a lot of fun stuff about why you like track."

"Thanks, Ivy, I chose track as my topic because it was easy to talk about. Reilly's speech was really entertaining, though. I had no idea he was practicing magic at home. He made everyone laugh with his card tricks."

LET ME TELL YOU ABOUT EPILEPSY

***

Nearing the end of the eleventh grade, Ivy, Gretta and Reilly were involved with different groups at school. Reilly with baseball, Ivy had begun rehearsing for a role for the next theater performance, and Gretta still loved to compete in track.

"Hey, I passed my written exam!" Reilly said, holding up his score sheet to Ivy and Gretta as proof, as he pulled up a chair to join them for lunch.

"Did your doctor give you the okay to drive?" asked Ivy.

"He sure did. Now that I've been off my medications for a year, my doctor cleared me to drive."

"I hope I'll be able to go off my meds someday, too. Fingers crossed," said Ivy.

Gretta also offered her congratulations to Reilly, except for a noticeable lack of enthusiasm that the other two couldn't help but notice. "You okay, Gretta?" asked Reilly.

"I think I'm going to be trailing you guys. I had a seizure last night. I don't think I'll be able to go off my meds for a while. My seizure only lasted a few seconds, but it was still a seizure. At least we'll all be together at the University of North Carolina."

"Right," nodded both Ivy and Reilly with conviction. The three had made a promise to apply to the same college. They couldn't imagine it any other way.

"I don't need to drive," said Gretta, "I'll live at the dorm. Driving costs too much money anyway. I'll be better off walking and using the school shuttle."

"At least we don't get drowsy on our medications, Gretta. Some day when we do drive, drowsiness won't be a problem and we won't have to switch to new medications. That's good news, right, Gretta?"

"Gretta, your seizures have gone way down over the past year or so. Your meds are working. Keep working on your dosages with your doctor. Frankly, I'm relieved that none of us are going to a college far away. I'm glad we're staying close to home. We'll all be near our families, and we won't have to switch doctors." Reilly said, trying his best to comfort Gretta.

"We'll study together. Most of our friends are planning to go to the University of North Carolina, too. We'll have a great time, driving or no driving," Ivy said.

"You're both right. It's just that I get down after I have a seizure. I've always told myself that someday I won't need meds. But when I get a reminder that epilepsy is still with me, I get discouraged. Most of the time, though, I'm grateful that my epilepsy isn't as bad as a lot of the people in the support group." Gretta said, giving it her best effort to sound upbeat.

"We have our whole lives ahead of us. And we've got each other. Because of you guys, I'm more excited about starting college," Ivy said.

"You're right, Ivy," Gretta admitted.

"Besides, I'm kind of scared about driving. People without epilepsy can be really dangerous drivers. People speed, they drive drunk, and they text. So, as far as I'm concerned, driving isn't the most important thing in the world, and if my doctor were to tell me I had to wait until after college to drive, I'd be just fine with that," Ivy said with conviction.

"I can drive you guys around anywhere you want. I promise I'll be safe," Reilly said reassuringly.

"And no texting," both girls shouted.

"Right, I promise," Reilly said.

There are over 40 different types of seizure. What seizures look like can vary. For example, someone may go 'blank' for a couple of seconds, they may wander around and be quite confused, or they may fall to the ground and shake. So not all seizures involve shaking.

Phenobarbital was introduced in the early part of the 20th century as a treatment for epilepsy. The ability to measure blood serum levels was also recognized as having value in this time period. The relationship between blood serum levels and effectiveness and also toxicity was also recognized.

Physician groups generally oppose mandatory reporting to their State's Division of Motor Vehicles, fearing that patients will not be forthcoming about seizures and, thus, be improperly treated.

The use of antiepileptic drugs does not prohibit an individual from driving a personal vehicle, but discontinuation of the medications is a matter of some concern, with some physicians advising patients not to drive or limit driving while tapering off or discontinuing medications.

***

Ivy hadn't needed to see Dr. Grant in over eight months, and she was now a Senior at Raleigh High School.

"Good morning, Dr. Grant."

"Hello, Ivy, it's nice to see you again. It's been a while. You look great, how've you been feeling?"

"I feel great. I've been involved in theater at school for quite a while and I really enjoy acting with my classmates. My theater teacher is great, too."

"I'm proud of you, Ivy. You've followed all of my recommendations, especially about sleep, nutrition and exercise, and I think it's paid off."

"Keeping a diary helped me stay on track and keep me motivated. I'm glad I didn't have seizures every week. I never really needed a service dog, but having Audie by my side helped me feel secure, especially at night. He's the best."

"Has Audie warned you about a seizure since your last appointment eight months ago?"

"No, in fact I've been spending less time with him because of all of my school activities. He hasn't acted anxious or pushed his nose on my calf at all. I haven't felt tingly, or spacey, or anything, and I haven't felt any side effects from the Keppra."

"Ivy, you haven't had any seizures for well over a year. Maybe we should talk about tapering your dosage and see how that goes."

"Really?"

"Yes. I think it's time we give it a try. I'll taper you slowly. If you experience any old symptoms returning, send me an email through your patient portal. I'll drop your dosage by 250 mg's. You can begin the taper tomorrow, if you like.'"

"I can't believe it. I could really go off of my seizure medication? You think I'm doing that well?"

"You've done very well, Ivy. But remember, I recommend you continue to take good care of yourself. Tapering off of your meds doesn't mean you can start eating junk food, using street drugs, or drinking alcohol. I want you to keep your overall health your top priority."

***

"Gretta, guess what. I saw my doctor yesterday. He thinks I should try tapering off my medication. Isn't that great? I started today."

"That's good news, Ivy. I saw my doctor yesterday, too. We talked about me going off my meds, but I don't feel ready. He told me to take my time and think about it. To be honest, I've decided to keep taking my meds for at least another year. When I told my doctor, he supported my decision. We're just going to postpone tapering for now."

"Gretta, all three of us are doing better. Reilly is already off his meds, and he's driving. He thinks he'll never have to be on his meds again."

"I'm glad he's doing well. He's driven me to my last couple of doctor's appointments, and he's a really safe driver."

"Maybe by the time all of us graduate from college, we'll have put epilepsy behind us, Gretta."

"Nothing would make me happier. But, even if that's not the case, all three of us know how to manage our seizures, how to tell others about it, how to ask for help, and what medications work for us."

***

"Mom, I'm going to miss Audie when I leave for college. Do you think he'll be okay?"

"Ivy, I'll give him all the love and attention he needs. Think of it as Audie retiring from his job as your alert dog. I've read that many licensed service dogs retire when they get older. Gunner and I will make sure Audie gets plenty of play time. Besides, you'll be home on the weekends, and the two of you can make up for lost time then."

During Ivy's senior year of high school, Audie spent more and more time with Gunner and Charlotte. Ivy was attentive to her dear Audie, but Ivy was busier than ever with rehearsing for her theater performances. Audie spent more time relaxing and when he needed attention, Mother Cole was the one in the household he knew he could count on. His belly rubs and kibble treats were always available, and he enjoyed catching a few extra naps between occasional barks at delivery men. Gunner, too, was busy with his computer games and baseball, but he always had time for Audie. His heart still melted when he got his face-licking, and Audie always got his kibble afterwards.

***

Ivy and Gretta were both admitted to the University of North Carolina and were dormitory roommates during their freshman year. Reilly lived in the dormitory wing next door. Ivy told Gretta once how Gretta had come into her life when she needed her the most, but ironically, Gretta knew deep in her heart that it was Ivy who'd saved her.

Ivy and Gretta were in several classes together. Reilly was in English and Biology classes with both. Ivy decided that science interested her most, and Gretta had already shown an interest in becoming a physical therapist.

Ivy successfully tapered off of her medications and remained seizure-free. Gretta decided to continue taking her medications, at least for the near future. Reilly remained a devoted friend to both and continued to be their de facto protective brother—through thick and thin.

Eating the Rainbow of Fruits and Vegetables

1 2 3 4 5 6 7 8 9 10 11 12 13 14 15

Across

3 Important to have a variety of this on your plate at each meal

4 Be careful not to eat too much of these types of foods

7 Should keep this calculation about weight below 25

8 Colorful orange and high in potassium

9 Strive to eat this many servings of fruits & Vegetables every day

11 White & sweet, but should reduce the added amount of this

13 Often argued as the only grain that is a complete protein, containing all 9 essential amino acids

15 Takes a certain amount of this to stick to your meal plan

Down

1 Living breathing part of us that turns over once every ten years

2 Colorful fruit and full of nutrients

5 These particular vegetables are high in nutrients

6 Use this quieting practice daily to help reduce stress

7 Good for your heart and high in fiber

10 Dark leafy green vegetable

12 Do this activity daily briskly

14 Come in saturated and unsaturated forms. Saturated should be kept to a minimum

Facts about Service & Alert Dogs

WORD LIST:

ALERT
BARK
BOND
CARING
FALLING
FOOD
LOYAL
PAW
SERVICE
SMELL
SOCIALIZED
STABLE
TRAINED

Epilepsy Quiz for Teens

1. An individual is given an epilepsy diagnosis after experiencing one seizure.
2. Doctors and hospitals can trace the seizure to a known cause.
3. In the majority of cases, epilepsy is controlled with medication.
4. Teens and children diagnosed with epilepsy, in the majority of cases, often outgrow their condition allowing them to live a normal life without medication.
5. One in twenty-six people in the U.S. will develop epilepsy at some point in their lifetime.
6. Three in ten people with epilepsy live with uncontrolled seizures because no available treatment works for them.
7. One in ten people will have a seizure in their lifetime.
8. Some people have a diagnosis of reflex epilepsy triggered by specific sensory inputs.
9. Some sensory input examples are: Flashing lights, music of a certain pitch, doing math calculations, and loud noises that are startling.
10. Lack of sleep is not a trigger.
11. Hormonal changes such as menstruation are sometimes a trigger to seizure activity.
12. Some prescribed, OTC, or herbal medications trigger a seizure.
13. A person with epilepsy can injure themselves further as a result of falling.
14. There are alert dogs that possess an innate ability to sense and alert their owner that a seizure is about to occur.

Surprising Facts About Driving

Across

2 Which gender are better drivers?

5 The most expensive car in the world.

6 A person who texts and drives is ___times as likely to have a crash than someone who drives drunk.

7 77% of vehicle crashes happen within _____ miles of the driver's destination.

9 _____driving is defined as any non-driving activity that occurs behind the wheel.

11 What is the color of car that is pulled over 2nd most often.

13 Sleepiness dulls your ________.

15 An estimated 1 in 25 adult drivers report having fallen ______ while driving in the past 30 days.

Down

1 _____drivers of cars and vans were involved in twice as many fatal accidents.

2 What color of car gets pulled over and ticketed the most.

3 ____while driving is riskier than talking on a cell.

4 Distracted _____ are the top cause of car accidents in the USA today.

7 ______, in slang usage, is sometimes used to define the applying of makeup while driving.

8 You must do this before starting to drive.

10 Road _____ is aggressive behavior exhibited by motorists that is extreme and poses an immediate risk to another.

11 Why do they call it ____ hour when no one moves?

12 ______ driving is a profound impairment that mimics alcohol-impaired driving.

14 AAA estimates that nearly eight out of _____ drivers demonstrated aggressive behavior when driving.

ANSWERS

Eating the Rainbow of Fruits and Vegetables

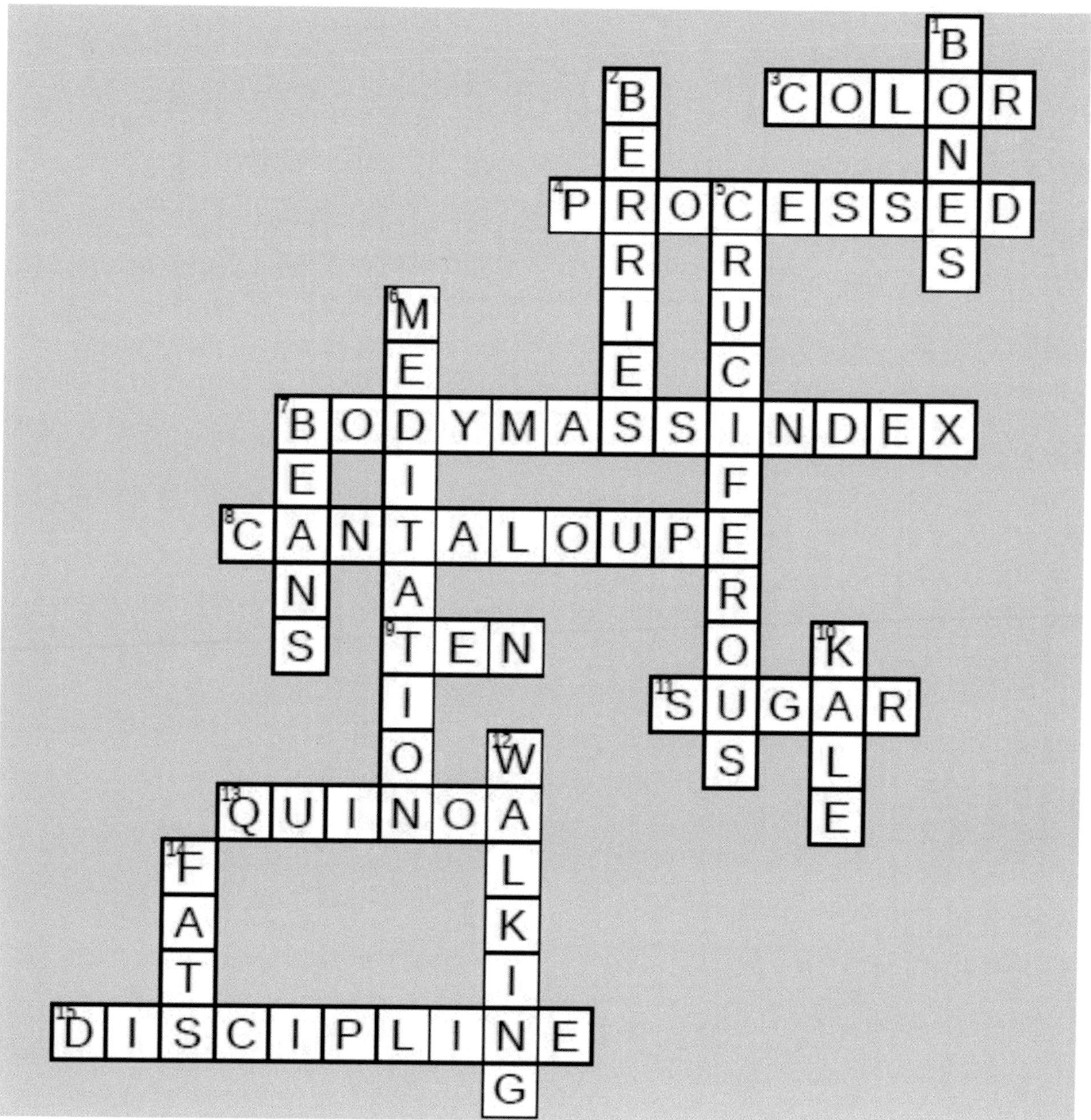

Words Related to Epilepsy

J G B R Q G N I H C T I W T C Y A S O O
Z D I A T S R I F S T R E S S C B M S M
V L Q U R T Q H U M C J G L B A S G V K
B A Z B E W V L R F C A K Q V D E E K R
B C A Y S K Y I R E A R U A C I N O L C
M O Y W Q I M E D I C A T I O N C R H E
J F Y R O M E M G M O D I E T D E J C X
Z T L G B C J Y R E G R U S E H P O S D
M L Y O P E E L S S M R S T R G N F Y S
B V F D H E A R T T E E N S S V Y A E D
I D F E S G N I H T A E R B U P H L D S
C E C C T E C V E V G F S L V T G L K V
W R O I D V D A J P U R S A O G Z I M E
B A N V O X V E U M I I G N I J Y N R H
H C F R N U L B K S O L I W Q T X G Y C
C S U E X R J N W N E C E D I A R Y X A
L E S S W Y A D S P H S J P H E L P Y D
I A I Y S E M O C T U O U C S W J B Z A
J X O T G N I R A T S A K E Z Y R U V E
Y L N G B C Z Y V T R I G G E R S I M H

Facts about Service & Alert Dogs

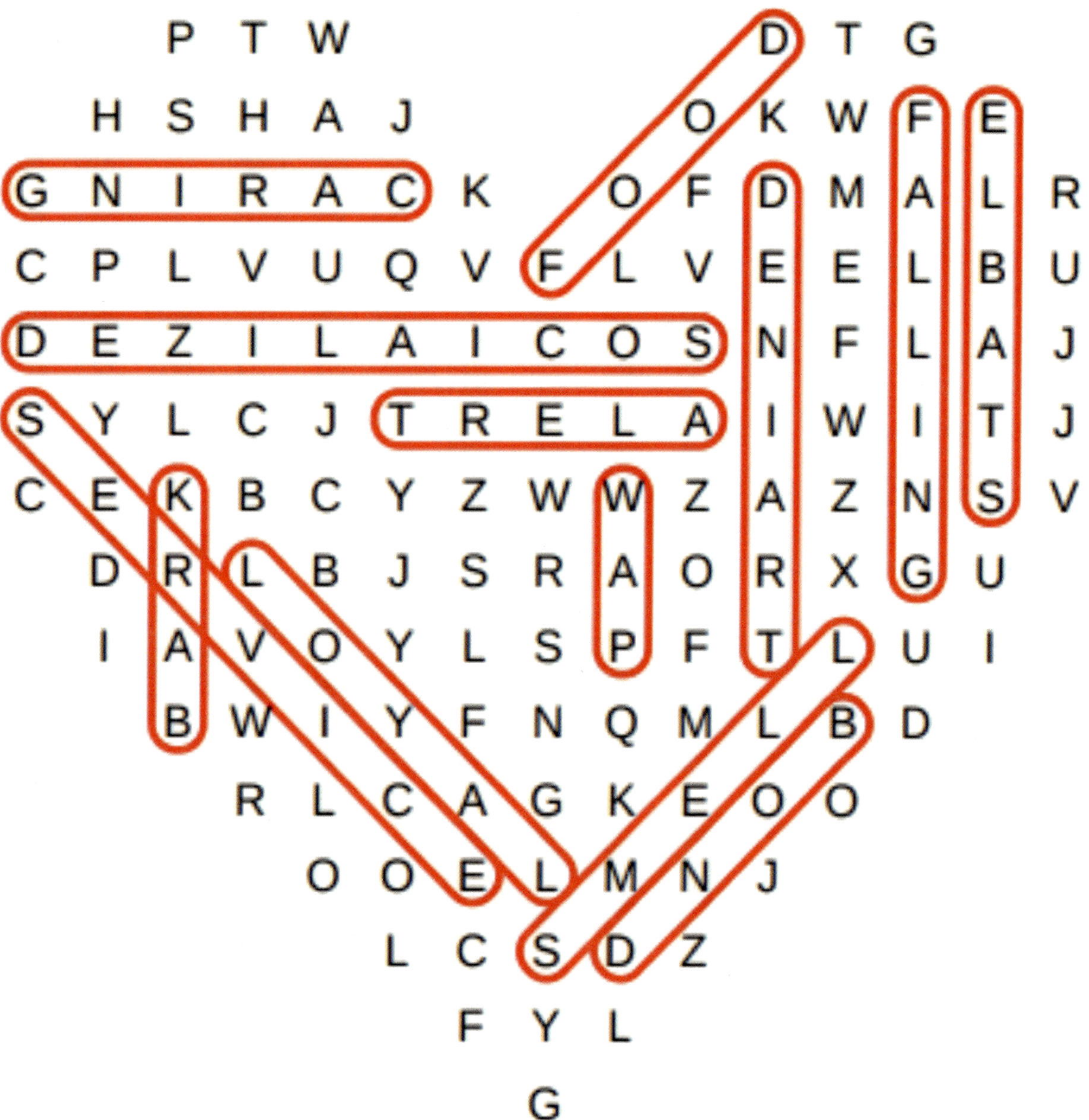

Epilepsy Quiz for Teens

1. FALSE
2. FALSE
3. TRUE
4. TRUE
5. TRUE
6. TRUE
7. TRUE
8. TRUE
9. TRUE
10. FALSE
11. TRUE
12. TRUE
13. TRUE
14. TRUE

Surprising Facts About Driving

ABOUT THE AUTHORS

Colleen MacFarlane is a native of Minneapolis, Minnesota. She is a genealogy enthusiast. Her first book, *Listening to Her Own Voice*, chronicles the life of her 2nd great aunt who emigrated to Minnesota from Switzerland in 1866.

Colleen enjoys reading and writing both fiction and historical fiction. She holds a Master of Arts degree in Counseling Psychology and an MBA in Personal Financial Planning. Her clinical experience and education utilizing both degrees influence the characters she writes about and the dilemmas they find themselves in.

Colleen has also authored several papers for a worldwide employee assistance firm on such current event topics as "Choosing a Financial Planner" and "Living in a 55+ Community."

Colleen has long felt that dogs enrich the lives of their owners. Her current dog tried feverishly to warn Colleen of her impending seizure by nudging her leg. With the assistance of medication, Colleen has been seizure-free for years, and her dog, Lucy, continues to be her alert dog, always by her side.

Dr. Bruce MacFarlane earned his doctorate in the neurosciences from the University of Pennsylvania. He earned his undergraduate degree in Physiological Psychology from Yale University. He spent thirty years in the medical device industry with a specialty in Regulatory Affairs. Bruce is a skilled technical writer, and assisted numerous medical device companies worldwide to obtain approval from the FDA so they could sell their product in the United States. As a young teen, he experienced a seizure after a hard bump to the head when using monkey bars at a playground. He was treated successfully with Dilantin. While still a teen, he successfully tapered off his medication and went on to college as planned and without incident. He has been seizure free without medication all of his adult life.

Ivy and Audie is dedicated to Gabby, Colleen's third miniature schnauzer, who died during an epileptic seizure. Colleen and Bruce reside in North Carolina.

Thank you to all readers who have purchased *Ivy and Audie*. Our book is available on Amazon. Colleen and Bruce invite all who read *Ivy and Audie* to consider posting a review.

Please visit www.colleenbooks.com to review all of her publications. Colleen maintains a monthly blog which includes several photos and excerpts from each of her books. In August of 2022, Colleen will begin offering one free PDF per month on her website for everyone on her email list. Topics are wide-ranging including: Recipes, crossword puzzles, articles with resources on genealogy, and numerous articles on a variety of financial topics.

Made in the USA
Middletown, DE
29 November 2022

16471617R00049